THE SINS OF SEVEN SERIES

KNEEL

DANI RENÉ

Warning

In a world of secrets, where sins are hidden from sight, people live their lives hoping that those around them never know what desires they conceal. The darkest needs, those that taunt just below the surface. Those they hide in the deepest recesses of their minds. Those things they don't admit to. The things they don't talk about. That's what this series touches on. You may find some of the subject matter disturbing, you may even look away, cringe, and gasp. But that's why I wanted to write these seven couples. These couples came to me with their confessions and I obeyed their need to have their stories told. The dark, depraved, the taboo. The things we may find tempting, alluring, and may even be turned on by it. That's what I wanted to write.

Each story is an interconnected standalone, delving into the relationship of the couples you'll meet. There will be sex, there will most certainly be foul language. And there will DEFINITELY be taboo subjects covered.

The Sins of Seven revolves seven couples who are so different in nature, in what their likes and dislikes are. They're each unique in desire, in their personalities, and even in the way they try to show affection. They don't love. At least, they don't think they do, they don't believe they're worthy of it.

Each story will make a point of focusing on one of the seven deadly sins.

Greed, Pride, Lust, Gluttony, Sloth, Wrath, Envy.

Although they'll be released in their own order, you'll be able to tell which sin, follows which couple and their journey to possibly find their happily ever after.

Please heed this warning.

This is a dark romance, suitable for mature audiences, 18+ ONLY. Strong sexual themes and violence, which could trigger emotional distress, are found in this story. Certain scenes are graphic and could be upsetting to some. This story is NOT for everyone. Proceed with caution. Discretion is advised.

"Most men pursue pleasure with such breathless haste that they hurry past it."

Kierkegaard

"To the women who

find strength in kneeling,

find love in anger,

find happiness in tears,

And ultimately find light in the dark.

NATE

Greed is my vice. A sin that leads to my addictions. One of the seven deadly sins to be exact. Perhaps greed didn't lead to my demise, but it did, in many ways, change me. My tastes differ from most men. I enjoy the tears on a beautiful rosy hued cheek. I revel in degrading women in sexual ways for my gratification and theirs.

Don't get me wrong, I'm not saying my tastes are right. All I'm saying is that there are women out there who come to me to be degraded. At thirty-six, I've had many slaves in my dungeon. A Sir to beautiful, intelligent, and submissive women who enjoy being called names while I'm fucking them.

In their humiliation, I command them what to do, while spitting out taunts at them. You'd be surprised how many get off on it. As if being called beautiful was wrong. In this world etched with darkness, that's where I find comfort. It's where I'm most myself. Where I'm allowed to let go of life's stresses, to see things in a completely different way.

Where I revel and play with my demons, other's shy away from their true, animalistic needs.

I've currently got a raven-haired beauty on her knees before me. She's being watched by three other dominant men while she kisses my shoes in exchange for an orgasm. I can tell she's needy because her breaths are ragged and I can smell her arousal. It drenches the room in a scent so intoxicating, the men watching have their dicks out, stroking themselves to the slave on her knees.

Like darkness feeds and preys on my soul, I do the same with curvaceous beauties. "Up, on your back. Open your legs as far as they will go," I command, my voice raspy with lust.

Her real name is Kristine, but in this dungeon, where devils come to play, she's called Fuck Toy. It's written on her stomach, just above her belly button.

Her smooth-shaven cunt is bared to me, the soft

pink flesh glistening. Picking up the champagne glass I brought into the dungeon only moments ago, I drizzle the contents over her mound, watching the clear, bubbly liquid drip down her folds.

"Please, Sir Nate," she begs.

They all plead at one time or another. Her thighs are trembling. Her big green eyes peek at me with unabashed need. I pick up the scrap of material she was wearing, a thong, pink and girly, yet there's nothing innocent about her. Kneeling at her cunt, I push the silk into her hole, fucking it into her like I would my cock. Her moans skyrocket through the room. The desire, lust, and darkness is palpable. A living breathing entity joining us in our depravity's.

I glance at the men. They're edging, bringing themselves to edge of orgasm to make their lust last. They're in awe of the woman who's allowing me to degrade her. "Come on your panties. Soak them," I grunt before clamping her clit with the metal teeth attached to the slinky chain, which is connected to the clamps on her nipples. She screeches in pleasure, pain, I don't fucking care. All I know is that I need to be inside her. "You love being a slut, don't you?" I ask, but all I hear are her moans and whimpers. The sounds vibrate through her and she shudders.

The three men to my left grunt as they find their own releases. I move to her mouth, gripping my thick cock in my fist and slamming it down her throat, gagging her.

"That's a good whore," I growl as my own release shoots through me. And like any good slave, she swallows every damn drop.

ONE

NATE

Taking in the city below me, I watch the lights flicker on as the sun finally dips below the horizon, leaving the sky in a deep orange glow. I've always found solace in the dark. Even when my addiction became something that threatened my livelihood, I would sit in the dark, looking out over the busy city and know that I wasn't alone.

Everyone at one point in their lives wants, needs, and takes. I've learned at an early age that people will do almost anything for something that's bad for them. Vices. We all have them. I bring the tumbler to my lips and take a long sip of the spicy cognac. I'd spent my teens hooked on drugs, and my twenties were spent gambling away my life. And now, in my thirties, I'm addicted to women and sex.

The darkness of my desires is where I found myself.

The real me. Where I came to meet the man that's somehow comfortable in himself for the first time. It happened the first time I degraded one of the girls I was fucking. In that depraved darkness, I knew where I belonged. In the world of BDSM.

It was the only time I was truly in control. The gambling stopped and I basked in my new addiction. Years on, I'm still here, still enjoying every moment.

Women come to me for the solace that I normally seek in the darkness. There's times I wonder how they can want me. A man who finds satisfaction in degrading them, but I've learned never to judge someone for their tastes.

When the lights in the building opposite turn off, I know it's time. She's on her way. Guilt ebbs through me, but I will it away by downing the dregs of my drink. I told her I'd be there at ten and I know she's just left work to make her way to the place I torment my slaves, submissives, whatever you want to call them.

Me?

I call them sluts.

Yes, I'm an asshole. I'm the man in the Armani suit

that your mother warned you about. The one who will steal your heart while fucking your body and when I walk away, I'll leave you in tattered pieces.

Picking up my phone, keys, and wallet, I make my way down to the parking lot that sits below the office building. As soon as I reach my Mercedes Benz, I press the key fob and it unlocks with a click along with the lights flashing. In the driver's seat, I settle back and start the engine to a soft purr.

With the car in gear, I head out onto the road, the long stretch that will take me to the club Seven Sins, which has become my second home over the past few years. A place where I can find what I need in the women that offer themselves to me. When I found out what my tastes were sexually, this was the first place I walked into where I finally felt free.

Being in the finance industry and having people know that you're a Sir who enjoys degrading women doesn't go hand in hand. But Mason and Carrick have set themselves up with a goldmine and I don't mind giving them my money when they've spent their time making sure that the club is discreet, the clients are vetted, and the surroundings classy.

"Mr. Ashcroft," the barman greets with a nod, setting a tumbler on the counter after I venture inside the club. My signature drink—a double brandy with one block of ice. Anything more would kill the taste, whereas this gives it a tease, making sure the flavor fills my mouth the same way a woman would when I eat her out.

Most men have no idea how to properly devour a sweet cunt. They have to make sure her toes curl, that her moans are so loud her throat burns from crying out your name. And if she isn't pulling your hair out by the root, then you're definitely doing it wrong.

Sitting back, I offer him a nod. "Thank you, Dylan," I grunt out, turning my attention to the stage. A woman steps out under the spotlight. The lighting in the club is turned down completely, attention on the podium. Allowing my gaze to drink her in, I can't help noticing her elegance. She's slim, striking, with a classic, yet alluring beauty. I know who she is. She's the reason I'm here tonight. The last name on my list. After her, I'll be done and the requirements of the agreement I signed will be complete.

Her long wavy dark hair the color of chestnuts—with thin golden streaks highlighted by the light above her head—hangs to the middle of her back. She's dressed in a floor-length red gown that hugs her curves with thin straps over her shoulders. My guess is that she's in her early twenties. I never know the ages of the girls I take on, I only know they're innocent to this world of depravity.

My gaze falls to her full lips. They're glistening with pink gloss. My dick thickens at the possibility of her kneeling before me with those same glossy pink lips wrapped around the base of my cock. Perfection. I'm almost done with my perusal of her when those big blue eyes—the same hue as a tropical ocean—meet mine from across the room. I make no move to show her she's made me as hard as a fucking rock. No. I keep still. Our gazes lock in a standoff. *You'll lose this one, darling. Trust me.*

A moment later, she breaks the link, dropping her gaze to the floor and greeting the audience. The small smile she offers the crowd isn't for them. I know it because she casts one quick glance at me, and then she's holding the microphone in hand about to announce the next show.

Tall, lithe, and exquisite.

A submissive if ever I saw one. Perhaps I can keep her. Turn her into a slave who will be there at my beck and call.

"Quite the stunner isn't she, Nate?"

I turn to find Carrick grinning like he's hit the jackpot. The beauty on stage opens her mouth and the voice that falls from her lips is sultry, sensual, and I'm immediately enamored with her. The couple who's going to teach the audience some rope work steps up on stage. Mason and Savannah. But they're not where my focus lies. It's on the dark-haired stunner.

"What's her name?" I ask, acting as if I don't know. There's one thing I can't let on, and that is that this is planned. Carrick doesn't need to know. Sipping my drink, I savor the burn, trying to calm my raging hard on by focusing on the feel of the amber liquid trailing its way down my throat.

"Evangeline, I call her Eva. She's an… old friend," he informs me but doesn't tear his gaze away from her. I have a feeling he means more than just *friend*, but I don't question him. "She's twenty-two in a couple of weeks. I've known her since she was sixteen. Also, beautifully submissive," he tells me with satisfaction and I know then that he's been with her.

If there's one thing Carrick knows, it's how to get to me. I've become a regular in this place and he knows my game, to get all new talent before any of the other Dominant's get their teeth sunk into the women. This time, he's got the upper hand. It's okay though, I never take them for longer than one night. And this will be no different I decide. This agreement is only for one night, to make sure my benefactor is happy with my work and move on. And that's what I intend to do. Any thoughts of more with Eva are only fantasy.

"Tell her to meet me in the black dungeon. I want to play." I gulp the last of my brandy, rising to full height while offering him my hand. Once we shake, he nods and heads toward the stage.

I don't wait. I head to the room where I'm about to devour the pretty girl. I shut the door behind me, shrugging off my jacket, I hang it on the hook near the mirror. This room is one of my favorites. It's furnished with a large king-size bed, red and black curtains which hide the two-way mirrors where people can watch me use the slaves.

It's got a wall filled with whips, chains, floggers, and a few other naughty torture devices. An old friend, Oliver, is a fan of this room as well. We've all got our different needs, his being pain. A sadist that enjoys both men and women. He does prefer men, but I've seen him turn a young woman into a whimpering kitten.

My kink is degradation. Humiliation. I love making girls cry, ensuring they feel like nothing, then soothing the pain I've caused by fucking them mercilessly. Over the years I've found myself with slaves begging for that treatment and in turn spent four long years with beautiful women walking in and out my dungeon. I've never kept one. Never wanted to claim a woman as mine. I've always leaned toward sharing. Even though I've had girls on my arm, I've used other's as humiliation. Which in turn only makes them want me more. I never understood it, but who am I to deny them what they need?

When I hear the knock on the door, I smirk with

satisfaction of what I'm about to do. The woman I know is sitting behind the mirror will get off my back, and the one that's about to be kneeling before me will take the edge off.

"Come in," I call to the door, not turning to watch her walk in. Always leave them wanting more. Aching and needy. That's how a woman should be. The click, a soft whoosh, and then another resounding click tells me she's inside. In the cage with the lion. A hunter and his prey. Now it's time to play my game. Her perfume wafts over to me and I can't help inhaling deeply. The scent is sweet, reminding me of cherries. "Take off your dress." My command echoes off the walls; I don't miss the gasp that falls from her cherry lips.

"Carrick didn't tell me you wanted a scene. I'm not ready to—"

Pivoting on my heel, I meet her blue eyes with a hard glare. "Did I ask if you're ready?" I stalk toward her. Reaching for her long dark hair, I grip it in my fist and tug her head back. Desire immediately swirls in her eyes and I know she's a submissive. A slave.

But can she handle degradation?

Can she handle me?

"No, Sir. I'm sorry for speaking out of turn."

"You will be," I inform her in a gruff tone. "Now, take your fucking dress off, slut. I want to see what I'm playing with tonight." I release her hair, stepping back to watch her slink out of the thin red material. As soon as it pools at her feet, I allow my gaze to trail from her plump lips down over her luscious tits, noticing how hard her nipples are, peaked behind the deep crimson sheer material that cups them. Her stomach is flat, with a small diamond adorning her navel.

The panties—which match her bra, sheer and see-through—show me the small landing strip of dark hair that sits on her otherwise smooth mound. *Fuck.* Her long legs are toned, her skin glowing a delicate bronze that looks like she's been on the beach.

Her heels are the color of a fine Cabernet, matching her underwear. *Perfect.*

"I want you on that chair." I point to the velvet armchair that's perfectly situated facing the mirror. "Drape each of your legs on either arm of the chair. I want you open. I need to see your cunt," I order with a no nonsense tone that will tell her exactly what I am—an asshole.

I'm brutal.

I'm rude.

And I don't give a fuck.

"Yes, Sir," she murmurs. I watch her stroll over to the seat in question. Rolling the sleeves of my shirt to my elbows, I admire the way she moves. Graceful and elegant. She's simply exquisite. No other toy I've been with has captured my attention like she has in the first few moments like this.

Once she's in position, I make my way to the curtain, tugging the rope which allows anyone who's watching to see what's going on inside the room. The blinking light in the corner of the window tells me there's already an audience and I know who's sitting there. One small nod to tell the woman on the other side the show is about to start and I'm turning back to my toy.

I plan on edging her until she's crying, until her tears streak her pretty face. Then she'll make herself come while I'm watching. When I'm done with her, she'll be utterly fucked. I don't normally spend much more time with the girls from my list, but somehow, I know I'll be taking extra time with Eva.

Feeling her eyes on me as I move around the room, I head to the wall and pick up the candle. Lighting it, I carry it over to her. "Do you like wax?"

"Yes, Sir." She smiles, not looking at me. Instead her eyes are trained on my shiny black work shoes. Setting the candle on the small table, I crouch down beside her.

"Look at me." Her eyes flit over to me, meeting mine with hunger burning in them. "Do you like sitting there with your cunt on display for those men?" I question, pointing at the mirror. Her cheeks darken with embarrassment and I find my cock hardening painfully.

"Yes, Sir." Her words are gasoline to my already blazing need. I'm the fire that's about to scorch her, leaving her in the rubble of my destruction.

"Rub yourself, one finger, tease those lips through your panties. I want you to make sure that scrap of material is wet with those delicious juices." Like the perfect slave, she moves her one hand down between her spread thighs. I watch in awe as her index finger glides over the material covering her slit.

Her eyes flutter. Her long lashes whisper over her cheeks as the pleasure of her finger heightens her senses. Her hips move, bucking against her hand as she strokes herself into a heated frenzy. The scent of her arousal hits my nostrils, taunting me and I know there's no way I'm going to let her get away without tasting every inch of her.

"Stop. Now shift the material out of the way, I want to see your pink hole." I gesture with my chin. Her fingers grip the now sodden material, moving it out of the way until I'm met with an incredible view of her tight pussy.

I can't help palming my cock through the material of my slacks, imagining sliding into that perfect little body. She's incredibly sexy, stunning, and even in this depraved scene we're playing out, there's an elegance to her that I've never come across. As much as I know I shouldn't want her, I can't help it. This is an agreement and I need to remember that.

"Such a pretty slut for me. Aren't you, Eva?" I ask, using her name for the first time since she's walked in here. Her deep blue gaze meets my dark one; desire dances in her eyes like a flame in the darkness. In our darkness. I want to give her everything she's pleading for with that one look.

"Please, Sir," she begs then. Her words set me off like a stick of dynamite lit to detonate everything in its path, and I know this woman is going to be my end.

"Put your fingers in your cunt, I want to taste them," I order while leaning in, waiting for her to get two of her long, delicate fingers wet. She slowly sinks them in, deep to the knuckle. As she pulls them from her body, she lifts them to my mouth, offering me the glistening digits. I immediately suck on them. The flavor of her races through my veins like a drug. Musky, sweet, and tangy.

"Do I please you, Sir?" Her question hits me then, slamming into my chest, gripping my throat. When I open my eyes to regard her, I find the yearning in her stare. She needs this as much as I do.

"You do, sweet slut. Kneel on the chair, I'm going to fuck you in front of all those men jerking their dicks while they watch," I inform her, knowing that I'm leaving out one important fact. There's more than just a few men out there. And if Eva ever found that out, knew who was there, she'd hate me forever for doing this.

TWO

EVA

His order turns me molten. I shift off the chair, kneeling as he requested. Since I walked into the room there's been an electric current racing through me. My blood is hot, my core is wet, and my mind is in a place of safety. How he knew I was a slave, I don't know. Carrick just told me an old friend of his would like to see me. He didn't mention what I was in for before I entered the room.

Memories of Carrick and I together taunt me. What we did. Even though he wasn't open about what this man wanted, I know Rick. I trust him with my life. I know he'd never send me to a man who would hurt me. He's been my savior for far too long.

My mind erases all thoughts of my past when I feel Sir's fingertips on the waistband of my panties as he slides them over my hips and down my thighs. His touch is gentle, but his filthy words incite desire straight to my core in the most deliciously dirty way. I learned early on that sex is something to be enjoyed rather than feared. I'd felt that familiar ache for the first time when I was thirteen. I remember touching myself, feeling that tingle, that jolt of need. Over the years, I kept it to myself, shy to talk to boys, that is until I turned sixteen. Until Carrick.

"Put your head down, rest it on the cushion, spread your legs wide. I want to see you. Both those pretty holes I'm about to use and fuck." The filthy way he speaks to me sets my body and soul on fire. I'm hungry, needy for this man who talks to me like I'm nothing more than a slut. Even though he's a stranger, it feels as if he knows me. As if when he looks at me he sees me. The real me. I've never loved someone. Never wanted it. All I want is for someone to know who I am deep down. To fulfill this need, this ache that I'll never be good enough for men like this. That's why I asked Carrick to allow me to come here, to work as his hostess until I find my feet in this dark and forbidden world I've fallen into. To perhaps find a Dominant worthy of giving me what I crave.

I know I'm submissive. I have always been. It was

only when Carrick taught me the right way, did I find out where my missing pieces were. Those small shards of the girl I was laid at my feet, and slowly with his help and guidance, I picked them up. Now, I hold them in my hand, waiting for the man who will finally show me how to put them together. The gaping hole in my chest that many have left barren is still waiting to be filled.

When the man behind me rains down a harsh swat on my ass, I can't stop the yelp that falls from my lips. "When I speak to you, answer me," he grunts, but it's not anger that laces his tone and weaves its way around my core, it's desire.

"I'm sorry, Sir," I answer, realizing I'm being stupid allowing my thoughts to drift to more than what this is. Men like him don't give girls like me love. They give us the pleasure we desire. They fill a need for us—the craving to be used—and then they walk away. I don't expect love from him, but it doesn't hurt to dream. To fantasize. Now as he swats my ass again, I revel in it. I make believe that it's just him and me. And with each blissful spank, I smile.

"Is my sweet slut getting wet? You're mine for

tonight. Aren't you?"

"Yes, Sir."

"Good slut," he murmurs with reverence. "Actually, I prefer calling you sweet slut, because your cunt tastes like cherries. Delicious."

People may wonder how I can enjoy this degradation. How humiliation can be a turn on, but it is so much more. Deep in my soul, I find freedom and a sense of self in this punishment. He needs me to obey him by degrading me to nothing, and I ache for him to use me and make me whole with the pleasure I know he'll bestow on me if I'm a good girl.

I know that once this scene ends, he'll care for me. A harsh swat with his large rough hand lands on the fleshy globe, left, right, again and again until I'm a whimpering mess. "Open that pert ass for me," he murmurs, low and gravelly, his tone rich and smoky like the finest brandy. I reach back, and obeying his command, I spread the cheeks of my ass for him. I can feel my arousal trickling down my inner thigh. "You're wet, slut," he remarks with pride.

"Yes, I am, Sir."

"Good girl," he coos.

Those two words are what every slave wants to hear. It means I've pleased my Sir or Dominant. I've given him what he needs, and now he'll give me what I hunger for.

"Thank you, Sir. I am here to please you," I whisper. I know there are people watching me right now. They're probably stroking their cocks wishing it was them in here using me like a toy for their pleasure, but I'd rather have him above me than any other man.

My mind is blank for a moment, my eyes closed in anticipation. That is until I feel him nudge my entrance with the crown of his cock. The warmth of him threatens to engulf me in its heat. He's not even an inch inside me and I'm already whimpering.

"I'm going to fuck you. This tiny cunt will take every inch of my cock. Do you understand me?" he says quietly for only me to hear. Before I have time to respond, he plunges inside me in one long stroke. His cock stretches me brutally. He's big, thick and hard. I cry out in pained pleasure as I release myself and grip the leather of the chair I'm kneeling on. His hand swats at my ass, hard and unrelenting. He's trying to punish me, but all I feel is pleasure.

His hips slam into me, pounding me like I'm a toy for his pleasure only. And I wish in this moment that it didn't have to end. I realize as the bliss of him fucking me sends jolts through my veins, I want to be anything for him. With a tight grip on my hips, he continues his assault. My clit throbs with pleasure, my moans and cries are a symphony of erotic gratification.

Our world is dark. It always will be. But in that darkness, I've found myself. Once you let go of all the fear, the control, the stress and let someone else care for you, it's addictive. Being a submissive, a slave, isn't about losing yourself. It's about finding the control you possess by relenting to someone else.

And as Sir's thick hardness penetrates my body, he takes over my mind. I've been with men before, but this is something else. His vile words, the way he commands my attention is something more. His hand reaches for my clit, pinching it brutally, sending shockwaves through every inch of my body. His other hand fists my hair, tugging the long chestnut strands, and my back arches, causing him to hit that spot inside me that detonates me into a million tiny fragments of pleasure.

"Come for me, sweet slut. Drench my cock in your honeyed juices," he commands, and my body obeys. My pussy clamps down on his shaft, pushing, pulling, needing more, and needing less. My thighs tremble as he uses me. He takes. And I allow him to.

Slowly, my body comes down from the euphoric high, and I find myself staring into those dark eyes that seem endless. An abyss of desire and hunger pin me with his gaze. I can't help blushing, and murmur the words he needs to hear. "Thank you, Sir."

He nods with a smile at my response. I've pleased him, but he's still hard holding onto what I can only imagine means an orgasm he wants to give me another way. "Lie back, I'm going to have some fun," he rumbles in a deep seductive tone. The man is an animal, but there's something in his eyes that make me want to know more. Who's behind the dominating force that is this stranger.

Once I'm settled on my back, he reaches into the pocket of his slacks, pulling out a vibrator. Small, pink, and curved.

"Open your legs wide, I want to see those slutty holes." I obey because the fog of desire he emanates has my body trembling for more. He places the small device on my clit and drives back into my pussy. His cock thick and hard, spreading me open, hitting that tiny spot inside my body which has my toes curling. When he turns on the vibrator, it comes to life on my clit, sending me spiraling. The force of his thrusts and the tingling of the battery-operated tease is too much.

"Please, please, please," I plead, and my begging is more of a chant. A prayer to the devil himself to let me find heaven in the hell of our dimly lit room. But he merely smirks. He thrusts, plunging deeply into me. I feel him in my soul as he owns me in that moment, and when I open my eyes to meet his, I beg him to claim me.

"Do you want to come, sweet slut?" he taunts.

I nod, biting my lip to keep from coming too soon. I know men like this; if I do, he'll punish me. And right now, this is all that I can take from him. He turns the dial up higher, sending me into orbit. Hanging on by a thread of sanity, my nails dig into the leather of the armrests of the chair, clawing my way from the dark hole of euphoria. I'm about to snap and I'm about to lose my fucking mind.

He spits on his index and middle fingers and I know what he's about to do. Use me fully. His free hand moves to my ass, finding the tight ring of muscle there. I tense, but he lifts a brow in question. *Do you not want me?* I nod. We're speaking to each other without words.

My legs are shaking as he teases the tight hole open, dipping into me, teasing me open. "I want this hole, too." His smile is feral as he tells me this in a voice that isn't his own. It's the beast inside he's unleashed on me. Two fingers fuck my ass deeper as his cock taunts my pussy. "Come. Come hard for me." He finally gives me the words I've been praying for, and I do. My body convulses as I feel liquid squirt from my pussy. "Mm, a pretty squirting cunt." He smiles in satisfaction as I drench him in my juices. That's when his body locks and he fills me with his hot release. I can't stop watching as pleasure paints his features. He's handsome beyond reason. A beautiful dark angel. And I know that he's taking more than my pleasure, he's taking my body and mind, and if he really wants it, I'll give him my heart.

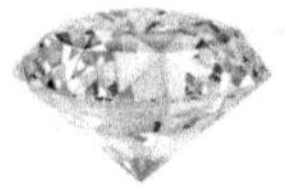

"This is why you were meant to leave when your daddy died."

His vile smirk is the only thing I can see. His face is so close to mine, I can smell the beer on his breath. The bitter malt he drinks reeks, his body swaying as he grips me harshly. He's never done more than bat me around, and I know soon, he'll lose control and really hurt me.

I'm fifteen. My dad died only six months ago and my mother returned to the home I shared with him, along with her filth of a boyfriend. They've taken over the house, left me to hide in the corners just to get away from them.

"You know," he sneers. The piece of trash my mother's been fucking regards me with hunger in his feral glare. "I wonder if you're as filthy as your mother is. Do you watch me fuck her at night?" He chuckles, his spittle flying from cracked lips. How my mother even thought this man was better than my father in any way is beyond me.

"Just let me go, if I don't get to school, they'll call her and tell her." I notice his eyes clearing as I say that. Thankfully, he

releases me. When he steps back, I can finally breathe.

"When you get home this afternoon, you're going to show me what's under that little skirt. And don't be late." His mouth curls into a sadistic smirk and his hand grips his crotch lewdly. I have to race out the house just in time to retch my cereal all over the flowerbeds that sit outside the front door. I know he's not lying when he says that's what he wants. He'll make me do it. And that's what scares me.

My eyes crack open and I shake off the nightmare. That wasn't the first or last time I was forced into a corner with the sick monster my mother brought home. I shove away the rest of the images that have haunted me for far too long and bring my mind back to the present.

My body is aching when I finally get up. Memories of last night taunt me and I find myself wet and needy. He left without telling me his name. After he'd come inside me, he closed the curtains to the viewing audience, lifted me in his arms and set me on the bed. Gently, he cared for me, stroking my hair, murmured how beautiful I was and then when I finally fell asleep in his arms, he left.

Carrick walked into the room, woke me up and told

me that the man said I was exceptional. When I asked more about him, my best friend only glared at me. I want to find him, to know him, but if he doesn't come into Seven Sins again, I have no idea how I'll accomplish that. Since Rick doesn't want to tell me who he is or even how I can contact him.

Pushing off the bed, I take in my apartment. The large penthouse is too big for me alone, but Carrick told me he's not happy with me living in a pokey little one bedroom shoebox, so he put down enough rent for me for the year. Twelve months of freedom until I decide if I want to move on, or stay in Chicago.

As I head into the modern kitchen, the silver appliances, and white tiles blink at me in the soft light of sunshine that's streaming through the windows. Once the coffee machine is turned on, I head to the living room to find my phone. No messages. No emails.

I left home at sixteen. After my father died, my mother stole everything from me. I was cast out like I wasn't even her child. It hurt, but she'd never been loving toward me. So, I ran with nothing. When I bumped into Carrick at a club, he took one look at me and told me I was perfect. I didn't know what he meant, but he was good to me. Fed me. Clothed me. And I begged him for more. In my teenage mind, I loved him. I gave him my body, my virginity. He took it the way I begged for it, hard and rough.

And when he spanked me, I pleaded for more. Over time, he taught me the beautifully erotic world he lived in. Leather, lace, chains, and wood. Whips and chains had never been so alluring.

The phone buzzes in my hand and I almost drop it. It's Savannah. Swiping my thumb over the screen, I smile while answering. "Hey Bunny," I giggle, using the nickname Mason gave her.

"Yeah, laugh it up, sweet girl," she responds and I can hear the smile in her voice. "I wanted to know if you'd want to have a girl's night tomorrow? My friend from school is in town and she's new to Chicago."

"Sounds like fun, I don't think Rick has me on to work tomorrow anyway."

"I'll handle Carrick, you just need to worry about a sexy ass dress," she says with confidence. I met her when I first walked into Seven Sins three years ago. It was the first time Rick allowed me into the club. Savannah is Mason's submissive. And Mason is a sex god if ever I saw one. He is Carrick's partner and the two of them have broken more hearts than I can count.

"You know I'm always up for spending time with you, Sav. What's your friend's name?" I ask while filling my mug with hot coffee, the rich, chocolatey scent taunting my taste buds.

"Peyton, she's gorgeous, I'm tempted to set her up with Rick," she confesses in a whisper. I never thought of Carrick being with anyone. He's too much of a playboy. Even after all these years, I still feel a twinge of regret that he didn't want me. Granted, he's amazing in bed, but for a long time I thought I was in love with him.

Nodding to myself, I realize Sav is waiting for my input. "Yeah right. You know that man can't stick to one woman. He's a glutton for them," I respond, sipping the dark liquid.

"This is true," she sighs in frustration. If there was death by sin, Carrick would be killed for gluttony. He devours women like a predator eating its prey. And the terrible thing is, they want it. "Okay, so tomorrow, seven?" Savannah's soft voice comes from the other end of the line.

"Perfect, I'll go shopping for a new dress," I tell her excitedly. She laughs, knowing that when I shop, I don't stop until I'm passed out under all the bags.

"I can't wait to see that gorgeous body hugged in a tight spandex." She giggles at that, and I can't help shaking my head. There's one thing about Savannah; she loves women as much as Carrick does, and Mason loves to share her with other submissives. I wonder how having an open relationship like that can work. Perhaps my jealousy holds me back from experiencing that, but deep down, if a man wants me, I have to be the only one he has. No sharing. It's too humiliating to me watching my man with someone else. Now, all I need to do is find said man.

"Okay, Bunny, go please your man, I need to get ready for the day," I tell her, padding back to the bedroom.

"Later, sweet girl," she says, hanging up.

I make my way straight to the closet to find something presentable to wear tonight. I'm working for a few hours, so I'll need something elegant. There are dresses overflowing my closet all courtesy of Carrick. My boss for all intents and purposes.

One day, when he does finally find a girl, she'll be one lucky submissive. He's got a big heart, big wallet, and a huge cock. Giggling, I shake my head and pull out the long silver gown. My mind flits back to the man from last night. As much as I try pushing him from my mind, I wonder if he'll be there tonight. And as I get my clothes ready, I know I'm going to dress for him.

THREE

NATE

The early morning sunlight streams through the windows of my office. My mind isn't here, it's still in that room with *her*. I'm not supposed to be thinking about her. It's done. I'm off the hook and I can move on, but I don't want to. When I left her last night, I told Carrick to look after her. I'd covered her in a blanket, wrapping her up after she'd fallen asleep.

Her body, her curves, the way her lips felt when I pressed a kiss to her mouth before I walked out without looking back. My chest aches, it fucking hurts, and even in the agony, I can't help smiling when I think about her. I'm turning into a fucking pussy.

My mind races with ideas, how I can get one more night. Just one. It wouldn't hurt. Would it? There wasn't any stipulation in the agreement that said I couldn't have a second taste. I'd finished what I set out to do. And if my benefactor never finds out, then it wouldn't hurt.

When I left Seven Sins after our scene, I walked out already needing to go back in and take her again, which isn't like me. I'm a one night, one scene man. I don't return to the same submissives. I've made the mistake before, when I got attached to a particular slave for two long years. I kept going back, requesting her. I became addicted. She became needy and greedy for my time. Wanted something I could never offer her. Not in the world I live. Love.

I've never been a one-woman man. They hate me for it, but that's not my problem. I'm too tempted by what I need. Too fucking twisted up in my own dark to drag Eva into it, but one more scene wouldn't make a difference. She'll be like every other slave I've played with. Fucking her out of my mind is one way of doing it, and if I degrade her enough, perhaps she'll hate me and it will be easier to walk away.

But last night was something else. Even as I take in the city below me, she's the only thing that's on my mind. All morning I've been at war with myself, convincing myself that it was a one off, but I'm a greedy man. Over the years my obsession, my dependence isn't far. My personality gives way to addiction easily. And deep down, I can't shake the need to know her. This is all going to blow up in my face, I know it, but I want her again.

With my mind made up that one more night will be what I need to get her out of my system, I pick up my phone, and hit dial on Carrick's number. We've known each other for a long time. I was the one who helped him when he needed the finance for the club, and when I made the move to Chicago to work with Asher, he was my point of call for help with my gambling addiction. Carrick's been a foundation, a friend, and I know he's someone I can trust with my life.

Four rings, and I'm about to hang up when I hear the familiar click. "Nathan, to what do I owe this pleasure?" The sly bastard answers in his thick English accent heavy with a smirk in his tone. Even though he's lived in America for almost ten years, he's never lost that lilt to his voice. Perhaps that's why women fall over their Louboutin's to get into his bed.

"Give me her number, Rick," I order, not bothering

with greeting him, but all I receive is a chuckle. The man is an asshole when he wants to be, and he's fucking good at it. I've become accustom to his personality and he to mine. That's why our friendship works. It's honest and brutal, just the way I like everything in my life.

"Why would I do a thing like that, Nate?"

"I want her. One more night." He doesn't respond, then I feel the vibration of my phone against my ear. When I pull it away, I notice a message from him.

"One night. If you hurt her…" He doesn't finish his sentence but I know what he wants to say. It's in his tone. If I hurt her, he'll kill me. Somehow, I don't doubt that. I've never asked about his background or why he left London, I don't want to know. But I know that it must have been something dangerous, there's just an air about Carrick Anderson that screams danger.

"Thank you, Rick. I owe you," I say, hanging up before he can respond with how much I probably do. When I open his message, I save her number on my phone. *Sweet Slut.* Even as I type the name I can still taste her sweetness on my tongue, my lips. Opening the message app, I tap out an order without giving her my name. That she'll learn when I see her again. For now, the mystery is more exciting. Anticipation. The crux of our world. I hit send and wait.

Me: Sweet Slut, I'd like to take you for dinner, for dessert I'll show you my dungeon. This isn't a request. It's an order.

I don't wait long for a response, and what I get in return makes me smile. I'm grinning like a fool.

Sweet Slut: Yes, Sir.

Two words and this woman owns me more than I can ever imagine owning her. I never thought I'd see the day that I'd even consider wanting to take a woman again and again, but with Eva, I feel that may very well happen. I'm playing with fire, I'm about to get burned, but I can't stop myself from diving into the flames.

I knew she wouldn't deny me. She can't. After the way she looked at me last night, I saw it flicker in her eyes. Need. That same dark desire that sets my soul alight danced in her blue orbs.

Me: Good girl. I want to watch you get dressed. Send me your address. I'll be there at five thirty.

Once her response comes through, I commit it to memory. Then, I turn to my computer in an attempt to focus on work. I have two new clients I need to get feedback to in the next few days. I pull up the documents detailing Mr. Grendall's finances. He's hoping to apply for finance which will see him setting out on a new business venture with his partner. The concern is his bank balance. This is where I step in. When he fired his previous accountant and contacted me, I agreed to work with him on this.

I need to focus. Going through all his financial transactions for the past five years. My eyes roam the figures on screen, but the only figure that's on my mind is the one of the woman who's caught my attention.

The day at the office didn't go as planned.

Yes, I attended meetings.

Yes, I impressed clients, but that's not where I want to be.

Every inch of my body aches to be inside Eva. Running my fingers through my unruly dark brown hair, I glance in the rear-view mirror of my Mercedes, and notice my eyes are swirling with lust, already hungry for her.

All day I planned, plotted, and I've figured out how to get her out of my system. We'll play a scene, one where she'll never be able to look at me with respect again. But before I do that, I'll take her to dinner. One date where I'll challenge her, tease her, and enjoy her. I'll make sure she knows who I am and make certain she won't forget me because I know without a doubt I'll never forget her. Once I walk away, it will be goodbye.

When I reach the door of her apartment at exactly five-thirty, I knock once and wait. I hear a shuffle from the other side and then the click of the lock. A soft whoosh sounds as she opens the door and I'm met with those blue piercing eyes.

"Hello." Her voice is timid, and a soft blush paints

her cheeks a rosy hue, cherries and innocence. A deadly combination of submissive sensuality and alluring beauty.

"Sweet slut," I murmur. I reach for her hand, tugging her close to me. I lean in and my lips find her cheek. I plant a tender kiss on the smooth skin of her cheek, which only serves to entice me more. Her body visibly shudders and she presses herself closer to me. Her heat warms me like I'm standing in front of a fire. "Do you like me calling you that?" I question, glancing down at her and meeting those blue pools. Her breath fans over my face as she peeks up at me under dark lashes, almost mocha in color. Against her tanned skin, she looks like a vision sent from heaven to drag me out of hell, only, I know there's no help for me.

"Perhaps," she quips. It's playful, bratty, and it makes my palm itch to spank her ass. A memory slams into me, one from last night when I spanked her. Those smooth fleshy globes of silky skin marked red with my hand print.

"Don't test me, sweetheart," I warn, lowering my voice. As she steps aside, allowing me into her personal space, I take in my fill of the apartment she calls home. "Did Carrick tell you to allow me in?"

"He may have mentioned that you're a friend and not a serial killer." She smiles, glancing at me with amusement.

"I may not be a serial killer, but I can be dangerous."

"Only to my body," she responds with a light tone, as if she's holding back excitement, perhaps a laugh. I follow her through the living room, finding that it's spacious. I wonder how she can afford a place like this. This block of apartments isn't cheap. Then it dawns on me. There's no way she's paying for this.

She leads me down a long hallway, lit only by the small downlights in the ceiling. A yellow glow that's reminiscent to candlelight. When we reach her bedroom, I can't help my surprise to find it neat and tidy. Most young women can be messy, unless she's tidied it up knowing I'll be entering her sacred space. There's a queen-size bed with dark blue sheets, almost midnight in color, reminding me of the inky sky. Her shoes are set out at the foot end, silver sandals with a slight heel.

A dressing table sits near the window and opposite

to that a closet is built into the wall with mirrored doors. How I'd love to fuck her while watching her face in those. A sight to behold. She strolls over to a hanger, which is perched on the hook beside the dressing table, approaching a long silver elegant dress. I can't wait to see her in it.

"I've set a chair out for you. I'm going to get dressed now and you mentioned you wanted to watch?" she says, not looking at me, but her confidence shines through. It's sexy, drawing me into her orbit like a moth to a flame. My gaze is glued to her hips as she sways them when she walks.

"Thank you, Sweet Slut. You are perfection in a tight little body," I remark, sitting back in the faux leather armchair which is situated beside the door. When she turns to face me, my chest tightens. I shouldn't be here. This wasn't part of the agreement and as much I'm breaking the rules, I can't stop myself. She slowly slips off the dressing gown, and when it pools to the floor, every sense of right and wrong leaves my mind. Her lingerie—a black corset, with a gold bow between her ample cleavage and a thong which matches with a bow on either hip—leave my mouth dry. Yellow, gold, the color of greed. One of the seven deadly sins. Perhaps this siren was made for me after all.

She plucks the silver silk dress off the hanger and allows it to fall over her body. The material hugs every one of her perfect curves. It drapes over her like it was painted on. She's covered in the floor-length silver dress. I'm speechless.

"How do I look, Sir?" Her words are sultry, meant to seduce, and they do.

Never have I seen a more exquisite woman, and I tell her so. "Exquisite."

She strolls to me after she slips on the pair of sparkly sandals. She'd be almost at my height in those heels, but she'll still have to glance up at me with those blue eyes. When I rise to take her in, my hands find purchase on her hips.

Meeting her gaze, I'm dragged into the arctic blue that greets me with shimmering desire, excitement, and happiness. My lips tingle with readiness to devour her. For a moment, I wonder if I should tell her how we met, or rather why we met. But today is the first and only time I'll have her again, so I decide not to. I make the choice to lie, just for a few hours more. What will it hurt? Even though I've learned first-hand that secrets are evil, they break down lives and relationships, but when I look at her now, I realize I can't say a word because to see her hurt would gut me. That thought scares the shit out of me.

"I'm nervous for tonight," she confesses shyly. In all her confidence, there's still a little girl hiding in there. A woman needing a Dominant to care for her. To take her places she's never even dreamt of. And in that moment, I don't see the mask she puts on for everyone else, I see her. The soul that's shattered, broken, and even though I know I shouldn't, I realize I want to be that for her. The man that will show her who she really is. Give her everything she needs and yearns for. Can I do this? The last time I took a chance with someone it ended badly. Worse than I ever imagined. But something tells me Eva is different.

A fleeting moment passes between us. My mind clicks into place when her lips purse, then turn into a small shy smile. My fingers dig into the soft flesh of her body, causing a soft moan to fall from her sweet lips. Yes. I can do this. God help me, I need to do this.

As long as she never finds out what I did, we can try. It's been a long while since I owned a slave. My own past is scattered with skeletons, but I offer her a reassuring smile. "Don't be nervous. I'm right beside you. You'll love my dungeon." I wink, offering her my arm.

FOUR

EVA

His confidence oozes from him, along with the spicy scent of his cologne, which lingers once he leaves the room. It's like a warm cloud of safety when I inhale deeply; I revel in it. I've only ever felt like this with Carrick. As much as I'd like to one day be owned, I've been rather shy to be with men. Something about this man who I still don't know, makes me feel like I can safely walk on the edge, and he'll catch me if I fall.

"What's your name, Sir?" I ask, a smile lifting my lips when his eyes twinkle with mischief.

"Nathan, and as much as I love it when you call me Sir, tonight you're welcome to call me Nate," he informs me. His voice is raspy, thick and decadent, and I recall last night, my thoughts drifting to the finest brandy.

And almost as if he knows that I can't resist his magnetic pull, he offers me a smirk that has my panties disintegrating the moment he gifts it to me, like a present at Christmas, but this is more priceless than a wrapped box with a red bow.

We make our way into the living room and I grab the purse which has my phone and keys. We move silently through the apartment, comfortable in each other's company, even though we know nothing about the other's personal life. Once I've locked the door, we take the elevator down to the parking garage.

I spy a beautiful Aston Martin sitting in a space, the lights blinking as we near it, and I notice the key fob in his hand. He opens the door, slipping his hand in mine, helping me into the cream-colored leather passenger seat of his car.

I admire his taste in cars while he rounds the front. I may not know too much about cars, but I recall my father telling me that once he made it big, he was getting himself an Aston. Daddy worked as a banker, he earned a good salary and we never wanted for anything, but before his death, he told me he'd put money away for me. He wanted me to one day be able to study, to have a life where I wanted for nothing. Sadness seeps into my mind then, the darkness of my past follows me. Even though it's been seven years since I lost him, that pain doesn't go away.

That's the problem with love. With caring about people. One day, they all leave. When Nathan slips into his driver's seat, he turns to me for a moment, placing his hand on my thigh. The connection sizzles between us, causing my sadness to dissipate for the moment, and has goose bumps erupting on every inch of my skin.

"If at any point you want to stop tonight, or want to come home, use your safe word, okay? I'll push you, but I'll never force you."

His words ease the tension and I nod. I knew he wouldn't hurt me. Not because he's a friend of Carrick, but because there's a kindness in his darkness. There's a flicker of humanity in his eyes, even though I see a rabid beast just below the surface.

"I know, Nate. Red if I'm at my limit and yellow if I'm nearing it, I've done this before," I tell him, nodding as he smiles, but a dark flicker of displeasure dances in his eyes. It makes me wonder if he's jealous. But as quickly as it appears it disappears, and I'm met with a warm, affectionate grin. Different to his sinful smirks and dirty stares. There are so many layers to Nathan that I find myself wanting to be the one to uncover them.

"I can promise you something right now, Eva," he caresses my name, as if it's the sweetest taste on his tongue. "You'll never need to use your safe word with me."

With that, he starts the engine, turns on the radio, and pulls out onto the road. Even though it's not late, it is quiet on the street. We easily weave through the minimal traffic, while I listen to the lyrics of the song currently playing. *Whisper* by Chase Rice taunts us through the speakers; his deep gravelly lilt sings sensually, heating my skin and sending a tingle down my spine.

Casting my gaze to Nate, I watch his jaw work as he concentrates on the road. The dusting of his stubble causes me to squeeze my thighs together thinking about his face buried there, in that spot that's now aching for him. *Sir Nate*. I like the sound of that.

Smiling to myself, I turn to face the road again, the lights like beacons in the dark, telling me this is right. It's where I should be.

"You okay over there, sweetheart?" he asks when the song comes to an end. Dark eyes flit over to me in question, and I nod.

"I'm just perfect, thank you, Sir Nate," I tease, testing the name on my tongue. Yes, I definitely like this.

"That you are, sweetheart," he replies, chuckling low in his chest, which makes me smile. The sound of his laugh is so different than any other man's.

So unique.

So Nate.

So mine.

The thought stills me momentarily, and I realize I want this. I want him.

Moments later, he pulls up to a valet for one of the most exquisite restaurants in the city, Everest. Situated on the fortieth floor, I've heard rave reviews about the food, the view, and the place itself. I watch Nate round the car, to find me waiting on the other side. His fingers protectively find the base of my spine, which causes a jolt of desire to sizzle through me the same way it does every time he touches me.

All my life, I've heard of those butterflies that girls

explain they feel when their crush is near, but I've never felt butterflies. Yes, Carrick and I had tension, sexual tension that skyrocketed when we were together, but this is different.

"Here we go," he says close to my ear as we step into the elevator along with a few other couples. The ride up to the restaurant itself is silent but the heat that's emanating from him is palpable. Once we reach our destination and the metal car spits us out into the foyer with the other people, I can't help my heart skipping. Dates in five star restaurants aren't for girls like me.

When we reach the blonde hostess, she glances up from her list and meets Nate's gaze. "Mr. Ashcroft, so lovely to see you again," she greets. The smile she gifts him is friendly, but her green eyes seem to hold his for a moment too long, glistening with something more. It makes me wonder if she knows him intimately, the same way I do.

"I booked my usual table," he informs her, ignoring her blush. She leads us through the rather large, but intimate restaurant, the soft lighting giving it an almost ethereal glow. People, mostly couples dressed in their expensive clothes—boutique dresses and designer suits—sit quietly at their tables, murmuring over candlelight.

When we reach the table, which sits neatly in the back corner, tucked away from everyone else, Nate pulls the chair out for me. I set my purse on the table and settle myself in the plush velvet seat.

He leans in, allowing his lips to whisper along my ear, causing me to shudder. "You're mine tonight." Those three words muttered under his breath make my anxiety dissipate. It dies just like a moth being sizzled by the flame.

I allow my glance to flit across the room as Nate rounds the table, seating himself opposite me. I can't help roving my eyes over him, taking in every inch of him that I can see. The man is beautiful. When we played out the scene, I thought he was handsome, sexy. But sitting here in a normal setting, he is utterly breathtaking.

The messy dark curls on his head look perfect for running my fingers through. The stubble that dusts his chiseled jaw looks as if it's only a day old, his skin tanned to a bronze, making him look like he'd been on vacation on a tropical beach. Shadows from the flame of the candle in the middle of our table dance across his face as he runs his coffee-colored eyes over the menu. My gaze drops to his hands, strong, with thick veins that rise from the golden skin. His long fingers, those same digits that I drenched in my arousal, hold the menu firmly, yet delicately. Everything about him is a contradiction, and I find myself even more enamored the more time we spend together.

"Are you going to sit there all night looking at me, Eva? Or would you like to decide on your meal?" he questions without looking at me, but there's a small grin on his lips that causes me to smile.

"I'm not sure what I'd like more, you or what's on the menu," I quip playfully, lifting the menu to roam my gaze over the list of items. He growls under his breath in response to my words, but that's all I'm afforded.

When the waitress appears, Nate offers a friendly greeting, asking her for a bottle of the 2009 Merlot, and two salads to start. As soon as we're alone again, he drops his darkened gaze on mine.

"Tonight, sweet Eva, I plan on feeding you both, a

lovely dinner and my thick cock," he vows in his low gravelly tone. His words have me shifting in my seat. "And while you're over there trying to ease the ache between your legs," he smirks knowingly and his deep brown pools drop to my chest then dart to my face, "I hope you're ready for dinner because I'm not like any other date that you've been with. Tonight, you'll have challenges. And for each one you complete, you'll get an orgasm." His words lower on the last two words, murmured with pure feral lust.

Straightening my spine, I square my shoulders and meet his gaze. "I can assure you, *Sir*," I breathe, watching as his eyes glow with desire. "I can meet any challenge you offer."

Before we can continue our torturous flirting, the waitress arrives with our wine and salads. Nate orders the sirloin steak, medium rare, with baked potato and stir-fried vegetables.

When the waitress glances at me, I ask for the same. She nods, jotting it down on her notepad, and then turns to leave.

As soon as we're alone, Nate fills our glasses with

the deep crimson liquid. I meet his dark eyes and they seem to swirl with hunger, dragging me into their depths. I know that I'm about to lose myself in the abyss that is Sir Nate… I realize then that he hasn't told me why he chose me last night, or even why we're here having dinner. "Why me, Nate?" I ask, innocently sipping the wine he'd poured.

"Why not you?" he responds with a question, lifting the glass to his mouth with a smile. I watch in tortured lust at the liquid that's left over on his full lips. He doesn't say anything until he's set the glass down. "Before we get down to learning about each other, I'd like you to do something for me. First challenge. Take my phone, go to the rest room, lock yourself in a cubicle. Sit on the toilet, lift your dress and spread your legs. Once you're settled, take a photo with my phone, I want one picture with your panties in place. Then I want a second image of you with your one hand on the sweet lips of your cunt. Be creative." He sets his iPhone on the table and sits back. I watch him lift his glass again, sipping the red wine as if he hadn't just asked me to take selfies of my panties on his phone.

"Yes, Sir." I smile, rising on my heels and heading to the ladies' restroom. To say I'm nervous would be an understatement, but I want to please him. I also want to show him I don't scare easily.

Once in the cubicle, I do as he said, step by step. My hand is shaking so much, I have to take the photo a few times before I'm happy with it. Deleting the extra's, I lock the screen. Once I've straightened my panties and dress, I head back to the table. Slipping into my chair, I find he's moved seats. He's now right beside my chair.

"All done, Sir," I inform him with a satisfied smile.

"Give me your hand," he grunts. I offer him the hand I know he wants. The one I used to shift my underwear to the side to get the shot he wanted. He grips my wrist, pulling my fingers to his nose. Taking a long deep inhale, he growls when my scent invades his nostrils. "Fucking incredible." He holds out his other hand and I place the phone on his palm.

He doesn't look at the photos. Not even acknowledging what I just did. We continue our dinner in silence, every now and then he asks me questions about my life, and I only offer what I can in response. My past hasn't been the easiest and I don't feel like bringing our lovely dinner down with the depressing tale of my early life.

"Eva, I don't normally do this," he tells me suddenly. We've just finished eating, and we're on the dregs of our bottle of wine. Even though he only had one glass, he's made sure mine has been topped up all evening.

"What? Date the girls you fucked?" I ask him straightforwardly while holding his intense stare.

He's silent for a moment before nodding in response. "Yes, I suppose you can say that. I mean, I'm not really a man that can offer you forever. I asked Carrick for your number for one more night with you. And I promised him that it's only one night," he tells me wryly, and I hear the regret in his tone.

Furrowing my brows, I wonder why he's so adamant this can't work. Perhaps he's married. My gut clenches painfully at the thought that I've been with a married man.

"Carrick isn't my father. He doesn't own me. Tell me something honestly. Are you married?" I retort hotly.

He snaps his gaze to mine. "No, I'm not that kind

of monster. I don't cheat. If and when I take a slave, it will be her only. At the moment, my tastes differ to what you're perhaps used to."

"And what do you think I'm used to?"

"Eva," he says in warning. "I like things… I prefer things casual. Would you be averse to me fucking another woman?" His question hangs in the air heavily, a lead weight on our rather lovely evening.

"Why?" I ask. Shaking his head, he doesn't answer me which only serves to infuriate me more. "I'm not a child, Nathan. Tell me. What is it that you like that's so wrong?"

His hand grips my thigh as his fingers painfully dig into the flesh. "Would you consider being with a man who loves to throat fuck other women to humiliate you?"

A gasp falls from my mouth in shock at his filthy words. I've always wanted to be the only woman for my Dominant. I don't like sharing, but as I stare him down, meeting dark eyes that are filled with… something. I can't make out what's in those eyes because they're a mixture of emotion that leaves me aching to say yes to him. Even though it goes against every bone in my body.

Turning my gaze away, I gulp the last of my wine, then look at him. "Perhaps not, I'd want to be your only toy, should you take me on," I confirm with surety seeing his brows lift in surprise. "Take me to your dungeon. If after tonight you feel we should not see each other again, I will accept that. And don't let Rick be the one to tell you what I want."

He smirks then, his hand beneath the table still on my thigh. Inching it up, he slides my dress up slowly, teasingly. Even though the material is floor-length, in no time, he's bunched it up to gain access to his prize.

"Stay still, can you do that?" he whispers in my ear. His seductive rumble shudders through me. I nod, biting on my lower lip when he reaches my panty-clad core.

"Can I get you anything more?" Our waitress appears at the moment Nate's index finger finds my clit. Nate's deep dark eyes find my face, reading the pleasure written on my expression like an open book.

"I think my pet would like a whiskey, I'll have one too," he tells her nonchalantly as his finger dips into my sodden core. My fingers grip the cloth covering the table, nearly ripping it off, along with the glasses and the empty wine bottle.

"Sure, is that all?" Her gaze flits between us, but I can't find words to respond. Nate's finger dips inside me, the soft sound of his ministrations sound loud in my ears. "Are you okay?" Our waitress pins me with a questioning stare.

"That's all!" I cry out a little too loudly when Nate pumps a second finger into me, finger fucking me while the waitress stares at me as if I've lost my mind. It feels like I have because my orgasm hits as she pivots on her heel, speeding away from our table. Nate's thumb finds my clit, swirling it like a toy, teasing and taunting it, causing me to bite down on my bottom lip to keep from screaming. As I come down from the euphoric high, I find dark eyes watching me. He smiles. Silent. Deadly. He's a predator and he's caught me in his trap.

"You remind me of a diamond—exquisite and resilient. Your radiance shines in a world dark with desire and lies. And even in the harsh light of our truths, where other's fade, you shine. Come again for me," he commands while his fingers take me higher, his words send me spiraling as I drench his fingers under the table in the middle of the restaurant.

Shockwaves of pleasure shoot through me. Gently, he pulls his fingers from my core, drenched in my juices. Placing them in his mouth, he slowly sucks them clean with sinful need dancing in his eyes. The waitress sets our drinks down along with the check. She doesn't speak, merely glances at us, then leaves with a tight smile pursed on her lips.

"Drink that, quickly. We're going home, I'm too hard to think straight right now, I need your sweet cunt on my dick." His order comes harshly, and I recognize the beast from last night coming out to play. I down the shot, feeling the burn as it makes its way down my throat heating my stomach from the inside out. My skin prickles; goose bumps rise on my whole body.

Nate throws a stack of money into the black leather bill folder where the check hides from my gaze. He picks up the tumbler and knocks it back before rising with his hand held out, which I accept gratefully. As I stand, my knees wobble from the orgasm that wracked through me only moments ago, mingled with the alcohol I've consumed. He slides his arm around my waist, pulling me into his body as if I'm his possession and letting me go isn't an option. The thought sets my heart aflame, my soul alight, and my mind races with the possibility of it all.

We make our way side by side toward the elevators. The ride down is drenched in silence, yet heavy with lust. When we reach the ground floor, the doors open and we step outside. The cool night air is chilly, but beside Nathan, I bask in the warmth he exudes. The valet brings the car around a few moments after we stepped outside. Once we're in the car, Nate makes his way out onto the road. His concentration is in front of him and his hands don't leave the steering wheel. I wonder if he's frustrated or just turned on. I can safely say that I've never been so needy before. Not with any man, not even Carrick. The ride to the apartment block where Nate lives is quiet, filled with sexual energy so thick and dark my body shudders with need for it.

He pulls up to a face brick building which isn't as luxurious as mine, but still has an air of money wafting from the entrance with the doorman and security.

"Come, my sweet slut," he orders, the first words

he's spoken since he ordered me to down my drink. We head toward the back of the building itself and step into the waiting elevator. Once the doors slide closed with a soft whoosh, the car takes us up to the top floor where we step into a long, dark hallway. Apartment 423 greets us with its black wooden door.

He unlocks it instantly, pushing it open for me to step inside. He follows, shutting the door behind us. When I hear the click, my anticipation seems to skyrocket and I'm already trembling. Tentatively, I step further into the living space and take in the modern furnishings.

The open plan living room opens up into a kitchen, which is decked with silver appliances, and a black marble countertop. The sofas are midnight blue, almost black, and velvet, with an enormous white rug that covers most of the floor. A fireplace greets me on the wall opposite of the largest sofa. Everything is black and white. No color. Not even on the walls. I've never been inside a place that lacked so much color. I want to say something, but I don't. Instead, I wonder how lonely he must be because this doesn't feel like a home, it feels like a place someone lives in when they don't plan to stay long.

He steps up behind me, his body cocooning mine. "Come," he murmurs in my ear, leading me toward the staircase which takes us up to the top floor. A short hallway boasts four doors. "I have two bedrooms, one guestroom and the main one which is en-suite. I'll give you a tour later. I'm just too fucking hard to think straight right now," he tells me with a rumble both feral and sexy.

He leads me to the end where a door the color of the wine we drank at dinner awaits.

"If you want to leave—"

"I'm a big girl, Nate. I know," I respond, cutting off his explanation.

He nods, twisting the handle, he shoves open the door, allowing me to enter the so-called *dungeon*. The room is swimming in soft yellow lighting that's both calming and peaceful. There doesn't seem to be any windows I can see, but when he walks ahead and tugs on a white rope that hangs against the wall opposite the door, black material swishes in the silence and I'm met with the city lights, inky sky, and silver moon. The stars twinkle against the darkness. "Wow," is the only response I utter. With the dim lights, the moon's bright light, the room itself is lit, giving me a view of the beauty that lies within the darkness.

"Take a look around. Ask questions. This…" he gestures around the room. "This is me."

FIVE

NATE

She doesn't respond. Instead, she looks around in wonderment, her blue eyes flitting across everything in the room. Having her here, in the room where I've brought so many slaves in the past makes me angry. I can't explain it, but I want her to be the first.

Anxiety still fills me. It's the first time I've brought someone here after… Shaking my head, I attempt to focus on the here and now. On Eva. Her body moves through my space as if she were always meant to be here.

For some reason, I need her to be the only one that's ever been inside the one place where I feel myself. Where I don't have to hide.

Yes, visiting Seven Sins does allow me that, but deep down, I can't unleash myself fully on the women there. This is where I rain down punishments, pleasure, and torture.

Her body moves fluidly through my playroom and I can't tear my gaze from her beautiful form. Her elegance is unparalleled. This is where she and I will enjoy each other one final time.

My sacred space.

The room itself is larger than even my bedroom. With the large oak bed against one wall, with four posts that allow me to bind a woman to each one while beautifully spread for my attention.

The large windows that sit just beside it, the toys, St. Andrews Cross, even the Orgasm Tower, they're all mine, custom made for me, materials, wood; I had a hand in selecting everything. The dressers along the opposite wall house my toys.

The en-suite bathroom is decked out for any woman's fantasies with creams, lotions, and body washes, bubble bath that's scented to any emotion you'd need. I've made sure this place is a heaven and a hell.

"I like this," she murmurs thoughtfully, breaking into my train of thought. She trails her finger over the long wooden beam in the center of the room. It's got rungs where a metal chain can be fitted and moved higher or lower. In turn, soft leather cuffs hang from the metal where I'd love to have Eva bound and hanging limp for me to use her as I wish. Or cuffs which would fit just behind her ass, so she's open and exposed to me. A spreader bar sits at the base for her feet, and a small clamp is perfectly positioned to hold a wand, for her pleasure or torture, depending on my mood.

"We can try that, if you'd like to."

She turns, looks me dead in the eye, and smiles. "What made you ask for me last night?" Her question is curious, almost innocent. I can't tell her. Can I? Would honesty make me lose her or bring her closer?

"You're beautiful. Why wouldn't I want you?" I ask instead. Not giving her what I know I should. Without a response, she nods, reaching for the thin straps of her dress. She slips the material over the smooth golden skin of her shoulders, allowing the material to fall to the floor.

Her body covered in black with those small gold bows. Her curves are exquisite. She steps out of her sandals, putting her at a small five four to my six feet, allowing me to tower over her easily. I watch her move elegantly around my playroom as she places her dress, folded neatly along with her shoes, in the corner near the door. The perfect damn slave. I can't let her go. I have to, but I can't. I refuse.

When she rises and turns to me, she immediately drops to her knees. "Use me."

Those two words ensure that my cock is hard as steel behind the zipper of my slacks.

"Look at me, Eva," I command, low and dangerous. If she knew what I wanted to do to her, she wouldn't have given in so easily. Her gaze drags up my legs, torso, and stops on my darkened glare. "Do you know what you're asking of me?"

She nods. Her legs shift, opening her thighs so I have a beautiful view of her panty-clad pussy. Her nipples are hard, peaking against the soft material that's covering them. Her delicate nature doesn't meld with the filthy woman baring herself to me.

"What happened to you?" My question is filled with more emotion that I should allow. I can't care about her. She's a toy. Fun for tonight. I promised Carrick one more night. Fuck, I promised myself.

"Make me yours," she murmurs, and then, as if she

can read my inner turmoil, she adds, "for tonight." As if she's already a part of me. Her gaze must recognize the emotions warring within my eyes. We watch each other for a moment. A predator, the prey, and a promise of something so much more if we are to do this. I know myself, I'm a greedy man, and she's the ultimate prize. A poison that can turn my life upside down.

All night, I've been at odds. I feel like I've lost my goddamn mind. Back and forth with what I should do and what I want. Her body trembles, and I know she wants me as much as I want her. It's written all over her face. "Who hurt you, sweet slut?"

"That's not something a man like you would want to know, Sir. This is one night," she tells me with confidence I doubt she really feels. Although her answer doesn't tell me what I need to know, I don't push. I haven't claimed her, collared her. If she were mine, I'd punish her for disobeying and not telling me.

However, she wants to play, so we'll play. I crook my finger, calling her to me. She rises effortlessly to her feet and pads over to me. Gone is the woman that was dressed elegantly only moments ago. The person looking at me now is an innocent, sexy girl.

"Take your underwear off," I order while taking a small step back. I watch as she slips the scraps of material from her body. Once she's completely naked to my gaze, I can't help smiling. Every inch of her is perfection. I'm fully dressed, she's bare to me. I grip her hands, tugging her over to the wooden beam that runs from the floor to ceiling in the center of the room. Reaching for the leather cuffs, I bind them around her wrists. "Have you ever played with toys? And I'm not talking about a vibrator?" I ask, looking at her.

"Yes, Sir."

I nod, pulling the metal chain, which in turn lifts her arms above her head, leaving her hanging from her wrists. Her toes just about touching the ground. "I'm going to test your level of pain and pleasure. After you leave here tonight, I want you to never forget this. It's one night." Once again, I affirm the lie that I know I'm spewing.

She nods in understanding, but I notice the way her eyes gloss over with unshed tears. Turning away, I head to the chest of drawers in the corner and open the top drawer. Grabbing a butt plug, lube, and a few other toys I'm about to have fun with, I head back to Eva. Her body is incredible. Her ass is plump and curvy, perfect to mark with my hand print.

Spinning her around, I help her to step onto a footstool, making sure she's secure, I place a hand on her lower back which juts her ass toward me.

"I'm going to put a butt plug in this luscious ass now," I tell her, keeping my voice low and calm. Once I've got enough clear liquid on the small silver plug, I spread the cheeks of her ass, emitting a low growl when I find her perfect puckered hole. "Have you had a cock in this hole, sweet slut?" I grunt out, twisting the metal against the ring of muscle.

"No, Sir," she murmurs, whimpering as I slowly tease it against the tight hole that's tempting me as it opens for my toy. As it slips into her body, she moans seductively. The heart-shaped jewel on the end of the plug shimmers in the dimly lit room. I rise, turning her to face me again.

Reaching behind her, I grab the clamps, which are attached to a chain. Three small rubber tipped metal clamps for her nipples and her clit. Leaning in, I suck one pebbled bud into my mouth, grazing my teeth over the taut rosy flesh. Once it's hardened beautifully, I clamp it, causing her to moan and shudder.

I copy the action on the other side, toying with her other nipple. Once both her sweet nipples are clamped, I kneel before her. Lifting my eyes, I meet her glistening cunt. I reach with one hand, spreading her smooth lips, seeing the tiny pink nub. As soon as the rubber pins her clit, she cries out.

"Please, Sir!"

"What? Tell me what you need?" I grunt, my desire is spiraling as I watch her shudder.

"I need to come, please?" she pleads, her words pained as her head drops back. Her pain threshold is perfect, not many women enjoy a clamp on their clit. Once I'm at full height, I kick the chair from under her feet, causing the chains to clink and tug on her nipples. "Oh, God, please?"

Ignoring her, I grab the spreader bar, and fasten her ankles to either end. When I'm done, I admire my handiwork. The woman is utter perfection. I don't know how I'll ever replace her. I'm about to blindfold her, but when she glances at me with those ocean-colored pools, I know I need to see them. To have her eyes on me.

Picking up the leather flogger, I stroll around her, feeling her gaze on me until I'm behind her. "You know, sweet slut, since last night when I fucked this sweet cunt," I raise my hand, allowing the tips of leather to kiss her porcelain skin. "I can't get it out of my mind." My words cause goosebumps to rise on her flesh. "I've been needing another taste. Another feel of your silky, warm hole," I growl, lashing her again and again. A whimper, soft and dick-hardening, falls from her mouth.

"Sir, Nate, please. Please?"

I reach her front again, lashing her with another swat right on the glistening core of her body. Which causes her to tug on the cuffs, her legs trembling, her sweet juices fill the air, and I inhale, taking my fill of her scent.

"Please? I love when you beg, slut. It makes me rock hard. Ready to drive into your cunt," I say, smirking with intention in my expression. "Did you enjoy being fucked in front of those perverts last night?" I ask, causing her cheeks to darken in embarrassment at my question. I know she did. She gets off on the humiliation the way I do. Each moment that passes, the war in my mind seems to lean toward keeping her.

"I need you please!" she begs again, pinning me with a pleading gaze. Her words are fuel, her body is temptation, and her pussy is my new addiction. Dropping the flogger, I shove my slacks off along with my dark blue boxer briefs. Her gaze falls on my erection, widening when she sees the angry thick steel.

Leaning down, I undo the spreader bar from her ankles and grip her ass. Her legs wrap around my waist, her drenched pussy at my cock. With one thrust, I'm balls deep inside the most decadent body I've ever come across. Her slick walls grip me, pulling me in deeper. Her tits bounce with each plunge inside her.

"Did you, sweet slut? Did you like being mine while others watched?" I growl; my words are breathless as I take her. "Tell me!"

"Yes! I did," her confession turns me rabid.

"You love being a slut for me. A filthy sweet slut. Don't you?"

"Yes, yes, please, please!" Words fall from her mouth, mumbles of unintelligible pleading. My hips drive up into her, slamming into her body. Needing her. Claiming her. Wanting more than anything to own her. To see her kneel with my collar around that slender, delicate neck.

"Look at me, slut," I grunt, thrusting so deep she cries out. Her gaze snaps to me; her arms flail as I fuck her, lifting her into the air. "I want you. Be mine." I shouldn't have said it, but the words are out of my mouth before I can stop them.

"Yes, I will. I want to. I want you."

"Good girl. Tell me what you need?" I demand, my voice hoarse from the grunts, growls, and moans. Our wet skin slapping against each other is the only sounds along with her moans and mewls. Our bodies move together, her hips against mine.

"Please, Sir. I need to come."

Her sweet plea sends my desire soaring as I reach for her clit, circling it, tugging the clamp and teasing and taunting it, until she's pulsing around my cock.

"Come for me, sweet slut. Come hard on your Sirs cock," I bite out, clenching my teeth to hold on until she's found release. I don't have long to wait because she's right there. My spine tingles, my balls tighten, and my own orgasm fills her moments later. And I know, I'm fucked.

SIX

EVA

"You're a fucking disgrace, Evangeline Gallagher," my mother's shrill tone echoes through the living room, causing me to wince. I skipped school, and of course, they called her to inform her that her sweet little girl wasn't in class.

They caught me making out with Lincoln under the bleachers. He'd had his hand up my skirt, his fingers delving into my wetness. Isn't that what all fifteen-year-olds did? Why was she so angry? It's not like she cares.

"Are you even listening to me?" she screeches once more, getting in my face. Her hands grip my shirt, tugging me back and forth. Her dark eyes, nothing like my blue ones, are full of rage. "Are you going to turn into a slut? Fucking anything with a dick?" She spits at me, venom flying from her words.

Tears spring to my eyes, and I will them away. I'm not a slut. I'm a girl. A woman. If I can find a man who is willing to take me like that, I'll be able to ignore her taunts.

I saw him today. The one with the suit and tie. He's handsome. His car is fancy and when I asked about him, one of the girls at school called him Mr. Anderson. I know his name is Carrick, I learned it from a boy who did some work for him. I didn't ask what work. All I wanted to know was his name.

Carrick Anderson.

I've made my choice. He'll be my first. And then he'll save me from this shithole.

A soft kiss on my shoulder jolts me from the dream still weighing heavily on my mind. Turning, I find the cocoa eyes of Nathan. It's still dark and I realize I must have passed out.

"Hello, sweet girl," he utters with happiness dancing in his eyes. Scooting up, I grab the sheet and cover my breasts. I don't know why. But for some reason, I feel nervous with him staring at me with so much emotion. "I saw all of you only a few hours ago, no need to hide anymore. Every inch of your beauty was mine to behold, beautiful," he says.

"Why am I still here?"

His frown creases his perfect forehead in confusion.

"Why wouldn't you be here?"

"You said that last night was it. One more night." Before I can get out of bed, his arm encircles me, tugging me closer to his naked body.

"I did. I wanted it to be the last night. But..." he trails off, his eyes closing as if he's in pain. "I can't, Eva. After last night, I just can't."

"Can't what? Nathan, I'm not—"

"I don't want to let you go. I've been up for hours, waiting on the sunrise to make sense of this... I don't know what to call it. I've been thinking..." He trails off, rising, he pulls me onto his lap. Onto his hardness that I again want to feel inside me. My body betrays me, rocking against his erection.

"Thinking?" I ask, as his eyebrow lifts in question at me blatantly rubbing against him.

"Yes, I have a proposition for you," he says, while his hips meet mine. Our bodies move like two pieces of a puzzle, fitting perfectly.

"Okay?" My response is wary. I know this man is everything that I didn't want at first, a man into darker kink than I'm used to. Someone who fucks other's because that's his need.

Desires. We all have them, some far harsher than others. I've never been someone who enjoys sharing, but this life, this whole world has taught me to never put a limit on something I've never tried. Carrick has opened the door for me, now it's my turn to step through and find out who I really am.

I know the only way I'll find my limits is by testing new and unheard-of desires. I've always enjoyed a few light spankings here and there, and last night brought me to a place where he was the only thing in my mind. Normally, the degradation would come, it would push me to a place where I found safety, but with Nathan, there is so much more—as if I *need* him to degrade me.

Yes, I've experienced humiliation in a sexual setting before, but Nathan is different. Even when he called me filthy names, his eyes told me something else. There was emotion there, which held me safe in the place where all my concerns dissipated to nothing.

Something snapped inside me last night. When he entered me, drove inside me, I felt whole. As if my shards had finally found their glue. As he held me up, connecting us in the most primal way, I felt as he if was holding all my broken pieces together.

I don't know if he can, though. Can anyone ever heal another person? I know there's a darkness in him that he hides. He's not yet allowed me to see his pain, his anguish that is so clear in the dark depths of his eyes.

"I want you. Three weeks. If you feel after that time you don't want to do it, then we'll tear up the contract. A business arrangement if you must."

"Three weeks?" I ask, my voice dropping to an almost unintelligible level. He nods, then reaches between my legs, his thumb on my clit, circling it and driving me mad. "I can't think when you do that," I moan, riding his erection along my now drenched pussy. Even though he's not inside me, I'm trembling.

"You don't have to think. I'll be your Dominant, I'll give you everything you need. You'll only have to worry about pleasing me."

My gaze snaps open then, I'm about to respond but he presses his thumb down on my clit, sending me spiraling and shaking above him.

"Do you like drenching your Sir's cock, sweet slut?"

He smirks. Satisfied that he's completely obliterated any refusal I had on my tongue.

"I have one request," I say when I finally find my words.

"Name it. It's yours."

I smile and lean forward, brushing my lips over his earlobe. "I want to play again in this room. Soon."

"Oh, darling we will," he tells me before I have time to straighten. Our eyes lock in a moment, something passes between us, but it's gone in the same moment it appeared. "And please remember one thing, Eva, I'll always call you sweet slut in our scenes, because you're mine. If ever someone calls you that, I'll kill them. You're mine. Okay?"

"Yes, Sir Nate," I smile, planting a soft kiss on his full lips.

"Now, my sweet girl, sleep some more. You're exhausted. There's still a few hours before sun up. We'll sign the contract later tonight, and we'll play again." When I move off him, I can't help blushing at the wetness I've left on his crotch. His eyes follow mine. When they lift to pin me again, he smirks sinfully. "Let's test your willingness to obey," he says. "Clean my dick."

Without a second thought, I'm on my knees, lapping at his softened shaft, tasting myself on him. He didn't come with me and I wonder if he's saving himself for later. His eyes burn into me, boring down on me in a way that's not demeaning, but as if he's worshipping me with a mere glance.

I rise, shifting off him once I've licked the wetness from him, and he smiles. "Good girl," he says with reverence as he shuffles lower on the bed; our faces are inches apart. "You're utterly perfect," he murmurs, his hand cupping my cheek as his tongue swipes across my plump lower lip. Once he's licked my arousal from my mouth, he rolls over, pulling me closer and kissing me deeply. His tongue delves into my mouth, hot, demanding, needing to be in control.

Our tongues dance erotically, tasting the other, reveling in the desire that pours from his mouth and into mine. Connected. Joined in an intimate way. I've always believed kissing is more intimate than sex. Fucking can be done without emotion, whereas there's no lie in a kiss. You can't join your lips to another's without feeling something.

My heart hammers in my chest, beating erratically and telling me to run. Warning me that this is a mistake and I need to be careful. But I won't. I know that as I straddle him once more, and he sinks deeply into my core, I'm fucked.

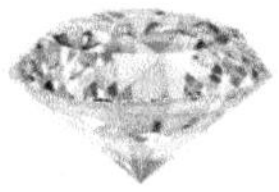

A gentle sound wakes me from the first dreamless sleep I've had in a long while. When my eyes crack open, I find the soft light of dawn shining down on me from the large windows of Nathan's playroom. The place he calls a dungeon, but after last night, I call it heaven. When I glance behind me, I find the bed empty.

Pushing off the bed, I pad over to the windows, taking in the beauty of the city in the orange glow of a new day. Sadness settles itself in my heart. I'm not sure if he meant what he said last night about me being his, I can only hope he did.

"You're awake," his voice comes from behind me, causing me to pivot on my heel. Carrying a tray of food, coffee, and fruit, he enters the room dressed in only a pair of boxers. He's so handsome, it hurts to look at him. His body is toned perfection. Golden skin shimmers as he saunters closer. His chest is smooth, free of any hair. Abs that call to me taunt as my gaze drinks in every inch of him. He's slim, yet built with a rigidness of a man that clearly works out a lot.

"I am." I watch as he sets the tray down on a small table, then makes his way to me. Big, strong hands grip my hips, tugging me closer so our bodies are almost one.

"Good morning, my sweet girl," he murmurs against my lips, pressing a soft kiss to my mouth. I can't stop my heart from pattering wildly against my ribcage at his words. Once again, he's the romantic man, the beast safely tucked away in the light of day. In the light of our truths.

"This… Last night," I peer up at him, meeting his eyes that are filled with honesty. "Did you mean it? When you—"

"Eva," he caresses my name. "I want you. I shouldn't. I know I should walk away and leave you to find someone who can give you a good life. Someone who won't hurt you. Because down the line, I'll hurt you. I don't want to, but I asked for three weeks and that's what I'll take. Then it's up to you to decide if you want to submit to me long term." He allows his words to sink into me and the silence around us.

"What if I hurt *you*?" I ask, knowing that if my past were to ever catch up to me, it could mean the end of something good for me. For us.

"You could never hurt me, Eva."

"Then let's try? I want to be with you. Have you ever had a girlfriend?" I question, but he chuckles loudly at that.

"No. I've never spent more than one night with a woman." When he utters this, I notice the flicker of guilt in his dark eyes, and instinctively, I know he's hiding something from me. Whether it's a past relationship, or another woman, something is hidden in his head, and I intend finding out exactly what it is.

"What makes me so different?" I wonder.

He stares at me for a long while, as if the answer is in my eyes. The way he looks at me feels as if he's seeing right through me. Deep into the darkness I hide.

"You're mine. That's what makes you different. My

beautiful diamond. You shine, in the dark where I find myself, you're the only light. Rare and beautiful. Mine." His words warm me, gripping my heart with fierce emotion, so deep, so goddamn painful that I need more.

"I want to play again," I tell him. He steps back, a smirk lifting the corner of his sinful mouth. The same mouth I want between my legs, devouring me like I'm his last meal.

"I do have breakfast planned, and trust me when I say that I wasn't planning on it being sweet and romantic."

"I didn't take you for the sweet and romantic type, Nate, but I trust you." I can't help giggling, however when I meet his gaze something dances across it so quickly and deceptively I think I'm imagining it. "What?"

"Nothing, let's eat," he responds, tugging me along and gesturing to the bed, where I settle against the black velvet headboard. Once he joins me, all the tension dissipates and we start on our coffees, toast, and softened cream cheese.

I can't help flitting my glance over to him as we sit in comfortable silence. Once my coffee is finished, I turn to him, moving the tray onto his lap. "I love cherries," I say, grabbing one, but before I can pop it into my mouth, he grips my wrist and shakes his head.

"Those are not ready yet," he growls. Glancing at the deep red fruit in my hand, I furrow my brow in confusion. They look perfect to me. Juicy, ripe, and ready to be eaten. "I want to you lie back, take those damn panties off and I'll show you just how I love to devour my cherries." Each word sends a rush of excitement and desire through me.

Quickly, I tug off my panties and drop them on the floor. When I lie back, I can't help meeting Nate's hungry gaze which roves over my skin. He takes in every inch of me as if he's committing me to memory so he doesn't lose himself on my slight curves.

"Open your legs," he orders. It's nothing close to the darkness that consumed him last night, but there's a no nonsense tone in his voice.

My thighs splay, baring myself to him. He grabs the small bowl of cherries. Popping one into his mouth, he sucks it until it's wet with saliva, and then he grips the stem and brings the cherry to my core. The cool red fruit teases my pink wet flesh and I can't stop moaning. Suddenly, he pushes the little cherry into my pussy, leaving the stem peeking out. "You see, Eva, I'm going to devour you and that sweet cherry dipped in your delicious juices."

I can't help my body pulsing at the filthy look in his eyes. He leans in as his lips crash onto my wet pussy as he sucks the flesh into his warm mouth. His tongue teases the fruit that's just inside me.

My hips lift involuntarily as he eats me like I've never been eaten before. His teeth graze my clit, biting down just enough to send a jolt of pained pleasure shooting through me, sizzling my blood with need.

Then, without much effort, he tugs the stem, pulling the bright red fruit from my body drenched in my arousal, and pops it into his mouth. "Delicious," he purrs, offering me a cocky wink, before inserting another cherry into me.

I'm moaning, begging and pleading for an orgasm, but he continues to devour me along with half the bowl of cherries.

When he finally sits up, his eyes burn into me with

one smoldering look. He shoves his briefs off, allowing his thick hard erection to jut out toward me. He nestles himself between my thighs and hovers over me.

"Do you want me, sweet slut?"

"Yes, I've wanted you since the moment I looked at you," I offer honestly. It's raw, it's scary putting yourself out there for someone you're still not sure will keep you.

"Good girl," he says, and with that, he slides into me, torturously slow. His mouth finds mine, his lips connecting with mine in a kiss that tastes of cherries and me. His tongue delves into my mouth, the same way his cock slides into my pussy. I'm wholly consumed in that moment. I've never once been so utterly owned by a man.

As our bodies move in sync and our connection grows, I know I'm allowing him into the depths of my soul I've kept hidden for far too long. It might not be a good idea, but in this moment, I have no choice because Nathan Ashcroft is stealing me. Bit by bit.

And there's not a damn thing I can do about it.

SEVEN

NATE

After breakfast, I stopped at her apartment so she could change into something other than a beautiful evening dress. Unlike most women, Eva was up the stairs and changed within twenty minutes. Once she joins me in the car, I pull out onto the road again with a smile on my face at the fact that I have her for three weeks. It's enough time to see if she's really the one woman who can withstand my needs. Most women can't. I don't blame them. And I know Eva said she doesn't like to share, so this will be a challenge.

"Where are we headed?" she asks. Her smile is bright and her blue eyes glisten with happiness that I want to have on her face forever.

"I was thinking about taking you for lunch, getting the contract from my office, and you're welcome to spend the afternoon reading it. It's not long, if you're comfortable with it, then we can play."

"And if I'm not?" she questions, glancing at me with a small frown on her forehead. Her words sit heavy in my chest. I didn't take into account her refusing. Having her walk away isn't an option.

"Then we'll negotiate," I answer.

She doesn't respond, and I don't offer more. Instead, I pull into the parking lot of a restaurant not far from the office building that Asher and I rent. Exiting the car, I round the front, opening Eva's door and offering her my hand which she shyly accepts. Her sweetness and innocence at times makes me want to collar her, but it's too soon. Far too early to even think about it.

As we head inside, the hostess who I've met months ago in Seven Sins walks up to us. "Nathan," she breathes, her gaze falling to Eva, then snapping back to me. "I-I'm uhm..."

"A table, Gabrielle," I order gruffly, giving her my Dominant voice, which causes her to blush, nod, and then scurry ahead of us. I can feel Eva's gaze on me, but I don't look at her. I can't. She must know that we'll come across women I've been with. But I don't understand why guilt sits heavily on my mind at that thought.

Fuck, she's softening me up. I can't do sweet and romantic. She'll have to get over it. I'll own her, she needs to submit to me. No questions asked.

At the table, I pull Eva's chair out for her, making sure she's comfortable before taking my own seat. Gabrielle sets the menu's down without a word. She knows not to speak to me unless I've spoken to her. Part of my rules.

"Bring us a bottle of sparkling water and the bread starter." My order is clipped, my lips pursed and all she can do is nod. As soon as I'm alone with my sweet slut, her gaze penetrates me so harshly, I have to meet it. "What?"

"She's your… she was your…" Her words fall to a whisper, tapering off. The hurt is distinct in her tone.

"She and I played, yes. I used her, and she enjoyed it. Is there anything else you want to know?" I grunt, slapping the menu on the table.

"I'm not yours yet, Nathan. You do not speak to me like I'm one of your dumb little slaves." Her voice lifts as the anger spurs her on. I want her bent over on this fucking table taking my whip for answering me in that tone.

"Let's get one thing clear, Eva, I'm an asshole. You knew that when you met me. This," I lift my hand, pointing between us. "Is just an arrangement. I may be sweet at times, but don't mistake it for weakness, I've always been a Dominant and no woman is going to make me soft with a flutter of her lashes."

"Oh, I have no doubt that you couldn't actually feel anything," she bites back angrily. When she pushes up, rising from the chair, I'm on my feet in seconds. "Don't." She bites the word out while pinning me with a heated glare. I watch in awe as she pivots on her heel, making her way to the restrooms.

If there's one thing she's mistaken of, it's that women do not order me around. Ignoring the glares from the patrons, I follow her through the restaurant and into the ladies' room.

"Leave me alone, Nathan," she says in a tone that's almost as commanding as the one I use on my toys.

Ignoring her, I grip her long hair, tugging her back against me. Pulling her into a stall, I slam the door and flip the lock. When I turn to her I see the fear in her eyes, but I also see anger. I press her against the door, wedging her between my body and the flimsy wood. "Do. Not. Ever. Speak to me like that," I grunt in her ear, hissing as she shudders. "I am your Dominant, and if you don't obey me I will punish you so badly, you'll not be able to walk for a week. Are we understood?" She doesn't respond immediately, but with one roll of my hips, I press my erection between the globes of her ass. "I asked you a fucking question."

"Yes, Sir."

"Good girl," I murmur, reaching to her front, I pull the skirt she's wearing, bunching it around her waist. My fingers find her pussy clad in the soft lace. My fingers taunt her heat, stroking her until she's clawing at the door. "Now what you're going to do is go back to the table, sit with me and have lunch. You are the one I'm with right now. Not any other woman. And if you don't sort this jealousy shit out, I'm going to fucking break you, Eva. I'm going to fuck you so hard, and so deep, your cunt will never be the same."

"Nate, please," she begs as my fingers dip under the

material of her panties. She's drenched.

"Do you like this, Eva? You like me pressing you against the door? I can do anything I want, can't I?" My words feather along her neck and my lips suck the soft skin into my mouth. I allow my teeth to graze along the skin, causing her to shudder against me.

"Yes, I do. I love it rough," she confesses when my teeth sink into her flesh.

Biting hard enough, I taste the delicious crimson liquid that dots my tongue. "Do you want me to unleash my beast on you, little one?"

"I want everything you've got," she gasps. Her words are filled with confidence and I wonder how much she can handle.

"Then tonight we'll see just how much you can take, sweet slut. I promise you, after we play tonight, you won't ever be the same. I'll break you in so many ways, no other man will come close to giving you the pleasure I can."

With that, I pull my fingers from her core and step back. I release her body, allowing her to sag against the door. Her breaths are ragged. When she turns, her

glistening eyes meet mine, and she smiles. "I can't wait."
She unlocks the door and makes her way out of the
restroom leaving me with a fucking hard on that could
cut through steel.

She's the perfect cut. A diamond that just needs
polishing and tonight I'll make sure she shines. With a
smirk on my face, I head out of the stall to walk past the
shocked woman glaring at me. Ignoring her, I pull open
the door and saunter back to the table, hoping nobody
glances at the bulge in my dark blue jeans.

When I pull into the parking garage, I turn off the
car and glance at Eva. She's been sitting silently flicking
through the contract that we collected at the office. We
make our way up to my apartment, once inside, she
settles herself on the sofa, pulling her legs under her, and
starts reading through the terms and conditions.

It's not a lot to go through, but it explains exactly
what's expected of her. She'll live with me full time, I
want her to be able to work or study without worrying
about money. I'll buy her clothes, food, toiletries, and

anything else she may need. When we head into my playroom, or the dungeon at the club, she will obey me no matter what I ask of her.

I've included that she's to wear a collar, even in the three weeks of us *testing the waters* so to speak. Everyone she comes into contact with will know she's owned. The collar will be a slim silver necklace with a pendant which will have an engraving on it *SS.*

The rest of it is standard lists of limits, both hard and soft. And that's where I know we'll argue. She doesn't like sharing, I do. I need it. Grabbing two tumblers, I pour a double shot of brandy in both, then make my way to her on the sofa.

"I thought you might need this," I offer.

She lifts her gaze, smiles, and then takes the glass. "Thank you," is all she says before dropping her head and continuing her perusal of the paperwork.

Deciding to leave her, I head to the terrace and take in the city air. It's a balmy evening with the moon already high in the sky. The sun is on the horizon, illuminating the air in a golden glow. I'm tense. I can feel the tightening in my shoulders.

I've never been in a situation where I've had a submissive read the contract. I drew it up a long while ago, when I was contemplating one, but that didn't work. I remember the day she walked out. She called me a monster, a vile animal and that was the last time I'd seen her.

That was the moment my life fell apart. The day love decimated me. Turned me into the monster she called me. And now, I no longer know how to be a man.

EIGHT

EVA

As my eyes scan the words, I find myself relaxing with each sentence. The limits are easy to work with. I agree to everything, each rule and regulation except one. I know it's a deal breaker. I know he wants and needs it. It's time to make my choice. To decide if he's the person that's going to push me outside that comfort zone.

Gulping the drink he offered, I push off the sofa and make my way through the living room and out to where he's standing. The tension emanating from him is palpable. A living breathing force that's alive and well, threatening to consume us both.

When I step onto the terrace, I find him standing by the railing, his torso bent at the waist, his hands clutching the tumbler so hard I fear it will shatter. His gaze is trained on the city below. I wonder what he's thinking. I can't stop staring at him, willing him to turn to me, to look at me with those dark eyes that seem as if he's searching for an answer that's not there.

I'm empty. I've always been that way. When I was seventeen, after I'd found Carrick, he and I had a fight. I wanted him and he didn't want me. Not in the way I asked, or rather, begged for. We'd become best friends who fucked, only, I was the one in love and he was in lust.

I ran that night, like I always do. One moment in time can obliterate everything you know about yourself, about what you think you feel. I walked into the main area of Seven Sins and found him. A man who willingly took me to one of the rooms and gave me what I needed. I asked for it and I was at peace for the first time in my life.

The next morning, Carrick forbid me to ever step foot inside the club again until I sorted myself out. That night, that man changed me, he showed me what it was like to live and die at the same time. And of course, Rick found out because he told me that someone had spoken to the stranger who'd taken me, found out what I'd asked for.

I've never felt the self-love people talk about. Perhaps that's why I enjoy the darker side of sex. It's the only thing I know. I've never had a man make love to me. And I'm afraid, if I ever do, I won't survive the aftermath.

"I agree," I tell him earnestly and I swear I hear him exhale. He straightens, turns, and stalks toward me. His eyes blazing, his smirk filthy and dark. "But," I say, causing him to halt immediately. There's a few inches of space between us which I want to close. "Tonight, I want you to take me to Sins. I want you to show me what it's like to share. To have you do what it is you crave so much. That darkness that swirls inside you, I want you to unleash it."

He's silent for so long, I'm not sure he's going to respond. Something tells me he wants to refuse me. I know why. I see it in his eyes. Fear. I'm asking him for the one thing that could possibly make me walk away from this.

"Look, if I'm meant to trust you, to submit, I'll need you to trust me too. Give me this, it's outside my comfort zone, it's a limit for me at the moment and you as my

Dominant need to push those limits. I want you to show me what it's like."

"*Eva,*" he finally says, pained. "I don't think I can let you walk away. If we do this, there's no doubt you will."

"Trust me?" I plead. This world is one that needs to be built on trust. And if that's not present, nothing will work between us. He reaches for me then, grips my hips and pulls me into him. Before I can say anything more, his mouth crashes down on mine, molding to me. His lips are warm, soft, and strong. Ever the commanding Master who takes rather than asks. Something about that calms me. His tongue delves into my mouth, seeking mine, testing for the submission with a simple kiss. And I give it. Freely, without reservation, only, I hold onto my heart for a moment. Just for tonight. Because if I give that to him right now, I'll never get it back.

When he finally pulls away, I'm dizzy. "I'll always trust you. That's not what worries me," he tells me earnestly.

"My submission is dependent on you giving me the benefit of the doubt. Show me my limits, break them down, and show me freedom. I give you my mind and body tonight." He nods then, but he doesn't smile. There's no indication of the man who I spent the day with. Not even an inkling of the same person that made me breakfast in bed, who took me shopping for clothes, or even the man who wined and dined me last night.

No, the man who now stands before me is the monster. The dark, depraved Master of the dungeon and he's about to lead me straight to hell.

He takes my hand, walks me into the living room and shuts the terrace door. We move through his home, directly for the bedroom where his king size bed waits for us, but we don't make it there. Instead, he spins around, pinning me against the wall. His body is hard in all the right places, every inch of him pressed against me. Without a word, he leans in, his lips on my ear as he feathers tiny kisses along the shell, causing goosebumps to erupt all over my body.

The heat of him is breathtaking. It's all-consuming. He steals all my thoughts as his hand grips my throat. The pads of his thumb and index finger put pressure on either side, and my vision blurs. *How can he even know?* My mind is a mess with questions.

This is what I want. It's what I need. That night when I tried breath play for the first time, it was the same thing, I had an out-of-body experience. I'd never come so hard. The rough, the violent way that man had taken me was consensual, but we played it out as non-consent. And somehow, even though I've hidden it from everyone, Nate's seen right through me. He's seen my soul.

"This, sweet slut, is not a game you want to play with me," he growls, pulling me out of my reverie. My lungs grapple for oxygen, my mind reaches for something solid, something to focus on so I don't pass out. But Nathan doesn't let up, he doesn't release me.

Reaching up, I claw at his wrist, digging my nails into the smooth tanned skin of his arm. He turns his head, allowing his eyes to meet mine.

"I'm a dangerous man, Eva. If you want breath play with me, you'll need to make sure that you give me everything. Your mind, your body…" A moment passes, just a short beat when both our hearts sync. I feel it. He feels it. And I know he's about to ask me for the one thing I just can't give him. "And your heart."

Ripping his hands away, he steps back, causing me to gasp a deep breath, again and again, painfully filling my lungs with air. "You're a fucking monster," I cough, spluttering as I fall to my knees. My hands splay flat on the floor. When I risk looking up at him, I notice the fear still present in his gaze.

"I know." He turns, leaving me in the bedroom still pulling in deep breaths as he makes his way to the bathroom. I wanted to play this game, this dark and dangerous game. A buzzing comes from somewhere in the bedroom and I realize it's my phone. Scrambling to reach my bag, I pull it from the purse on the bed and swipe my finger over the screen.

"Hello?" I sound breathless; my voice is raspy.

"Bitch, are you okay?"

Savannah. Sighing, I flop onto the bed. "Yeah, I'm good. What's up?"

"Tonight, the club? Did you forget?"

Shit. "I did, I can't make it," I tell her, cringing at the thought of explaining to my best friend that I'm about to submit to a man. At least, put him up for consideration. After tonight, I'll be able to see if I can handle his world.

"Does this have anything to do with the hunk that asked for you two nights ago?" It's been almost three days that I've been swept up in Nate's world, but it feels like longer. Like weeks, months even.

"It does."

I hear her sigh. "Do I really have to beg?"

"No, Savvie, I'm not Mason, you don't have to beg," I respond with a laugh. "He's taking me to Sins tonight for a scene. We're going to… well, I'm considering submission, and I've asked him to show me his worst."

"What?" she screeches from the other end of the line. "Are you serious?"

"Yes."

"Does Carrick know?" Her question throws me off the excitement and anxiety of what I'm about to go through tonight, and I realize I don't want to tell Rick. Mainly because he'd try to talk me out of it. But I also don't want him to know what's going on in my personal life.

"No. And he doesn't need to. Carrick Anderson doesn't own me."

"I'd like to see you tell him that to his face. If I'm

not there, please tell me you'll record it?" She giggles. Savannah is not a woman who giggles, but this time I have to admit, it is funny.

"Yeah, okay. I have to go. I'll talk to you tomorrow. I'm sorry I can't—"

"Please, gorgeous, you get your kink on. I want to hear all about it. And I'll have a drink for you, okay? Bye," she says and hangs up, leaving me smiling as I push off the bed.

"Eva," Nate's voice calls to me from the bathroom. When I turn, I find him dripping wet with a towel tied around his taut waist. Small droplets of water trail their way from his smooth toned chest, to the dips and peaks of his abs. The V muscles that point to the bulge behind the white fluffy material taunt me, and I lick my lips involuntarily. He strolls over to where I'm standing, my eyes drink him in, savoring the beauty that is Nathan Ashcroft. "I'm sorry," he starts. "I'm an asshole. I really don't know how to do this. To be…"

"You don't have to apologize. I wanted it. I've… I'll get ready," I mumble, pushing past him, but he's too quick. He grips my wrist, stopping me from making my way to the bathroom.

"Look at me, Eva." It's an order. I can't disobey, so I turn to him. "What happened to you? Who hurt you?" His voice is strained. Concern filling his tone, but there's no way I'm about to tell him about my past. The questions he poses come with the answers I can't give him.

"If this is going to work tonight, I'll need you to let me do it without talking about my past. Once I've signed the contract and that's what you want to hear, I'll tell you. But tonight, I'm not Eva Gallagher anymore, I'm just your sweet slut." Ripping my hand from his grasp, I race to the bathroom, locking myself in.

I press my back against the door as I try to pull in calming breaths. My past—the ugliness, the horror. I can't tell him. There's no way he'll want me if he knew how damaged I really am.

NINE

NATE

Eva Gallagher. *It can't be.* My mind swirls with the words she just uttered. Shock slams into my chest so painfully, I can't breathe. Three long days I've known her, and I didn't think to ask her last name. Now that she's just spat it at me, the guilt weighs on me, dragging me into the abyss.

"Nate? Nathan!"

Her voice cuts through the turmoil. I can't tell her. She'll hate me.

"What's wrong?" she demands.

She's in front of me before I have time to react. Her body is close to mine, her hands on my shoulders. Where our skin touches feels electric. I blink repeatedly.

"Nothing," I rasp. My voice is thick with emotion, fear that she'll find out. This needs to end tonight. She needs to leave. I need to fucking walk away before my whole world comes crashing down because of this one woman.

"Are you sure? You look like you've seen a ghost," she says quietly. "I'm sorry I freaked out, I didn't mean to—"

"Eva, just get in the shower, please? I want to leave soon." Her gaze implores me for more, for affection, but I can't give it to her right now.

"Okay," she finally appeases me, nodding.

Once I'm alone, I grip my phone and hit dial on the number that's haunted me for far too long.

"Nathan," she answers. Her voice is ice-cold, racing through my veins like poison.

"Why didn't you tell me about Eva? About who she was?"

Her cackle comes from the opposite end of the line, as if she's happy that she's completely and utterly destroyed someone. "I sent you to humiliate her, not fall in love with her," she tells me in her rage filled tone. "Did you, Nathan? Is this your heart or your cock talking?" Another shrill laugh echoes through the speaker, causing my blood to boil with anger.

"You're an evil fucking witch. Are you proud of the games you play with people?" I bite out harshly, but I know she won't be affected. Her dead heart doesn't beat, it doesn't feel. She's as rigid as a fucking corpse.

"Listen to me, Nathan, and listen very clearly. You were meant to walk into that room, degrade the little bitch and walk out. Happiness isn't in her future, and if I find out you're still seeing her, I'll fly over there and make sure the job is done myself. And don't for one second doubt that I'll make sure everyone knows what a sick bastard you are and what you did to Emelia. Do I make myself clear?"

Running my fingers through my wet hair, I tug at the strands, pulling it just to ground myself. I've never felt rage like I do right now. I did this. I fucked up my life, and now I'm about to do it to Eva.

"Nathan—"

"Yes, I understand." I hang up before she has time to say anything more. Slamming my phone on the nightstand, I exhale a deep breath.

"I'm ready," the sweet tone of Eva comes from the entrance to my bedroom. Dressed in a small red lace pair of panties, a matching bra that cups her breasts perfectly. Long dark hair hanging down to the middle of her back.

"You're perfect, Eva. Come here," I order. She obeys immediately, padding over to me. Once she finally reaches me, I cup her face in my hands. Her blue eyes peek up at me through those long dark lashes. "Never forget this, you are utterly beautiful. I can't imagine why you'd want me, and I hope after tonight you don't hate me." The words fall from my mouth, I can't pull them back. I agreed to let Eva go only moments ago, but each time she pins me with her innocent stare, I find myself crumbling. Fuck the consequences.

"I can't hate you because I asked for this. In order for me to accept the contract, I need to know you at your worst."

Nodding, I lean in to place a kiss on her full lips, and then I step back to allow her to get dressed. I stopped at a small boutique on the way back to mine and bought her an outfit for tonight. I didn't think she'd want to go to Sins, but since it's sensual and sexy on her slim frame, I know she'll be the center of attention. We move around my personal space as if she's always been there. As if she belongs there.

Once we're both dressed, we head down to the car with my anxiety following us as we slip into our seats, and I make my way out onto the road. It's silent, except for the music that's playing mainly as background noise. The only reason I put it on is to keep my mind focused on anything other than what I'm about to do. She asked for it. Begged me to show her what I enjoy. Fear ebbs and flows through me like a river, back and forth, taunting me with her walking out the door.

"You seem more stressed than normal," Eva remarks, as I pull into the parking lot of Seven Sins. The building is nondescript, nobody who passes here will know what it really is. From the outside, it looks like a gentleman's bar, but once you walk through the black velvet curtains, you're met with the dark depravity of the people who prefer the sadistic side of sex.

"I don't want to scare you off," I lie. I've become so used to lying to people around me, it comes easily. There's one thing I can't do, though, and that's look her in the eye and do it. She'll see right through my lie.

"If you say so," she retorts, exiting the vehicle before

I have time to respond.

Sighing, I push open the door and follow Eva to the club door where the two bouncers are poised with grim looks on their faces.

"Mr. Ashcroft," one of the bouncers says with a slight nod.

"Good evening, gentlemen. Eva will be joining me this evening," I tell them, allowing my fingers to find the base of her spine, trailing small circles there protectively. I don't miss the relaxing breath she exhales.

The other bouncer unhooks the red velvet rope, allowing us inside. We easily pass by the security checks and head straight for the bar. "Nathan," someone says from behind as soon as I place my order. When I turn, I find Carrick. I offer him my hand. "Good to see you," he says, smirking as he shakes my hand, his gaze falling on my date.

"Hi, Rick," Eva greets, smiling. Rising on her tiptoes, she feathers her lips over his cheek. It's a friendly gesture, but I feel jealousy boiling in my blood anyway.

"We're using dungeon three. I want the blonde on the stage," I inform my friend, gesturing with my chin to the beautiful girl that's introducing Mason and Savvie for their show.

"Olivia," Carrick calls, his gaze pinned on the blonde for a moment before turning back to me. His next conquest. I can read the man like an open book. He looks to Eva again and smiles. "Savvie and her friend were going to have drinks out tonight, but she mentioned you may want to join them after…" His words trail off for a moment, flicking those honey eyes to me before looking at Eva. "She was wondering if you'd have drinks with them later. I'll lock up to the public early since it's a personal party."

"Sounds good. Thank you, Rick," Eva responds. "I'll see you later," she tells him with a small smile.

"Yeah," he grunts. The threat is clear in his eyes when he looks to me again. "Have fun."

Once we're alone, I order a bottle of champagne from Dylan who's minding the bar, and we make our way to the back. Dungeon three awaits, either I'm about to fuck everything up, and lose the woman who's wanting to give herself to me, or she'll see the real me and want me even more. I'm hoping for the latter, but I can already tell when we step into the room and the other woman is

already there that this isn't going to be an easy feat.

TEN

EVA

As soon as we step inside the room, it suddenly feels too small. I can't be angry with him because this is what I want. Stepping further into the space, I take her in—blonde, beautiful, and curvy. She's dressed in a sleek black dress and heels that put her at my height.

"Hi." She smiles, but I can't bring myself to answer her.

"Eva doesn't like you, Olivia," Nate rumbles from behind me. I don't look at him. I can't bring myself to look at his face. He sets the bottle on the table and I hear him crack the seal and pop the cork.

Three glasses. Three people. I'm about to be hurt, degraded, humiliated, and it's all my fault. "Do you want me to leave?" she asks. The bitch who's going to get fucked by the man I want to kneel for.

"No, you're here to entertain me. Not her," Nate

explains callously. And so, it starts. He's no longer mine. This is the monster I asked for.

A click sounds against the wall and I know we're not alone. The green light flickers in the corner. There's an audience.

"Okay…" Her voice falls silent, wary even.

"Eva, I want you naked. Sit on the sofa, you'll watch," he orders harshly. I swallow the lump in my throat. This is one of the most difficult things I've ever done. I know it's a scene, I can call out *red* at any point I want, but my stubbornness won't allow it.

I slip my shoes off, and then my dress, which pools at my feet. Once I'm naked, I settle on the sofa. The next few moments feel like I'm having an out-of-body experience. Nathan stalks toward the blonde, handing her a glass of bubbly liquid. She sips it tentatively, her gaze flitting between him and me. My nipples harden when he reaches for her hair, gripping it and tugging her head back.

"Are you submissive, toy?" he growls at her. She tries to nod, but can't fully move with the hold he has on her hair. "Get on your fucking knees, get that champagne in your mouth and don't swallow. You're going to suck my dick."

He shoves her to her knees. When she gulps the bubbling alcohol, I watch her hold it in her mouth. She peers up at him, watching as he unzips his slacks, shoving them down his thighs. Once his cock falls from his briefs, he turns to me with a wicked smirk.

"Are you watching, sweet slut? This pretty little toy is going to swallow my cock."

The ache in my chest tightens as he grips her head and pushes his shaft into her mouth. His head drops back in pleasure when he hits the back of her throat. Dribbles of champagne fall from her lips as he continues fucking her mouth.

Tears burn my eyes. The need to blink, to allow them to fall, is at the forefront of my mind. But I don't. That's what he wants. He wants to humiliate me. He grunts as his hips slam against her face. Her hands grip his thighs, and I watch in pain, shock, and anger, as he uses her.

Suddenly, his body locks and I know he's coming. His release slams into him and he moans in pleasure. The sound causes me pain. She gave him the pleasure that I am meant to give him. When he pulls free of her mouth, he drags her to her feet and pushes her to the table. "Bend over," he tells her. He crooks his finger at me, calling me over to them. "On the table, she's going to eat you out. Do you like girls, sweet slut?" he taunts.

Shaking my head, I finally blink the tears, allowing them to fall. The salty emotion rains down my cheeks, burning as they make their way down to my chin and finally dripping onto my bare breasts.

When I look at Nate, his eyes are black with depraved desire. Lust hangs in the air and I wonder how I'm even considering wanting to submit to this man. Someone who wants to hurt me, who finds pleasure in making me cry. I settle on the table where the blonde is bent over, my legs on either side of the dark wood. Nathan picks up the champagne, pouring it over my tits, stomach, and down to my pussy.

"Eat her cunt, toy. I want you to make her come. She doesn't like girls, let's see how she gets off from your mouth on her." He chuckles darkly. The beast is out to play and my heart won't survive this, so I lock it away safely.

Our guest leans in, her gaze filled with apology, and I wonder why until I swipe at my face, finding it drenched. I didn't realize I was crying so much. I watch her mouth find my pussy and she starts licking at me, lapping the alcohol that's drenched me along with my tears.

"That's a beautiful sight. My sweet slut's tears make me hard," Nathan says. He steps up to me with his erection at full mast. He grips it in his fist and strokes it against my lips. "Open up, baby, you're going to suck me off now. Show her you're mine."

His words shock me. My gaze snaps to his, and he nods. There's no malice, only emotion. Through my agony—and embarrassment of making a girl drench her face in my arousal—I find the man I've been with for the past few days. Nathan is back and the beast is safely behind bars. I take him into my mouth, reveling in his pleasure that's sending desire zipping through my body, and I can't help moaning. "That's my sweet slut," Nate grunts as his fingers fist my hair. He shoves my head back and forth on his shaft. Using my mouth like he would my pussy.

He continues his assault on my face, fucking my throat painfully. Spit drips from my lips, down my chin. Tears, mixed with saliva, champagne, and my arousal are being lapped up by our blonde guest. I can't see through the blur of motion, but I feel her fingers enter me and I moan with Nate's cock in my throat which in turn causes him to growl.

"You're going to make me come," he tells me, but doesn't relent his harsh movements. My nose against his crotch, his cock filling my mouth and throat. Then Blondie bites down on my clit, and I let out a muffled shriek around the thickness, which sets Nathan off.

Hot jets of his release fill my mouth, sliding down my throat, and I do what any good slave does. I swallow it all. Every damn drop. He rips me off him, leans in, his mouth at mine, and then he kisses me. His tongue delves into my mouth as he tastes himself on my tongue. We kiss for what feels like hours before he finally breaks contact with me to look at our guest.

His cold eyes fall across her. "Get dressed and leave. You're done."

Her mouth falls open, but she doesn't refuse him.

Instead, she moves quickly, grabbing her clothes. She pulls her dress on and makes her way out the door. I sigh, relief causing me to sag onto the table, but when Nathan pins me with a glare I realize we're not near done.

"Thank you, Sir," I tell him, but he only smirks.

"Get on the bed, on all fours."

I move hastily from the table, walking on wobbly legs to the bed. I climb up, positioning myself on my hands and knees. I don't look back. I don't want to see what he's doing. I hear shuffling, and I shut my eyes. I know he won't hurt me, but something more is coming, and I have a feeling it's going to be worse than what he's just done.

His hand lands harshly on my ass, causing me to yelp. The clink of the belt sounds around me as if it's in surround sound.

"This is going to hurt, sweet slut," he warns before he rains down a swat with the thick leather on the smooth skin of my thighs. Another one lands on both fleshy globes of my ass, and I can't stay silent any longer. My cries echo off the walls. One. Two. Three. It feels as if I'm about to pass out from the agony, but then I hear the belt drop with a loud clang, and then he's above me, pushing me onto the bed. One hand grips my throat. "This is what you wanted isn't it?"

"Please, Nate—"

"Beg me, sweet slut. Cry for me. I want those pretty fucking tears," he snarls in my ear, his words coming out animalistic and feral. I thought the beast was taking it easy, now I know he's out, and he's about to demolish every part of me.

"Nate, Sir, please?"

"Yes, slut, I'm going to fuck your ass, hard, deep and fast. It's going to hurt. Perhaps you'll bleed." His chest vibrates with a rumble as he pulls me up, facing the mirror where I know there are men watching. Men who are getting off on my pain, my tears, and my fucking humiliation. In this moment, I hate Nathan Ashcroft with every ounce of my being.

His free hand grips his shaft pressing between the cheeks of my ass teasing the tight ring of muscle, but not entering me. I claw at the bed, trying to get away. Wiggling my hips, I manage to shift out of his way, but his grip around my neck tightens, my vision blurs, and I glance at the mirror. The green light flickers. They're there, but they won't help me.

"Do you want this?" he asks.

I try to respond, but I can't. Then his fingers of his free hand find my pussy, cupping the wetness roughly. Then he dips one digit into me, he guffaws from behind me.

"So fucking wet, sweet slut," he says with reverence. My body wants this. It needs this rough handling and I knew he'd find me drenched for him. He maneuvers us until he's behind me, the crown of his cock teasing my slick core, wetting him in my juices before he nudges my puckered hole.

Then I realize why he put the butt plug inside me last night. He was getting me ready. Before my mind can work out what to do next, he slams into me, causing me to screech in pain. It burns, sears me from the inside out. Nothing I've been through physically can compare to the agony that shoots through every fiber of my being. Then his fingers taunt my clit, tugging it, tweaking it as my body trembles, the pain that was present only moments ago turn, twist, and shift into something else.

His hips move slowly. Soft lips find my neck and his deep growl emanates through my back. No words. Just a feral, basal need. He pulls out, then eases back in. My body responds, it aches, it drips, and it squeezes him deeper. And that's when all my emotions spiral into one spot between my thighs and I find pleasure in his movements.

Pleasure and pain.

My mind is blank.

All I feel is him.

He's consuming me.

His hips slam into me, in and out, he fucks my ass while he fingers my pussy. My fingers claw at the sheet, but I don't want to get away. I want to stay right here, beneath him, taking him. The grip I've got on the material causes my knuckles to turn white. My body is limp, I'm a rag doll. A fuck toy for him.

"That's my girl," he coos in my ear. "Take my cock in your sweet ass."

His words heat my blood. His fingers are drenched in my juices, his cock deep inside my ass. "Fuck you!" I spit angrily, I'm playing the role. It's a scene. He wants it, I need it.

His hand on my throat tightens, stealing the tiny space I was breathing through and leaving me digging my nails into the mattress. My toes curl as the pleasure envelops me in its strong hold. "Come, Eva. Drench your Master's cock, you filthy little slut," he grunts.

His vile dirty words send me into the dark abyss of euphoria. I hear nothing. I'm soaring.

Somewhere along my flight, I feel him empty himself inside me. My lungs pull air in short deep gasps.

"Good girl. I'm here," he whispers reassuringly, allowing me to enter into a form of subspace and I know I'm safe with him. I'll always be safe with him.

I'm used. I'm done. I've kneeled. He wins.

Warm arms surround me.

Soft touches.

No more pain.

No more pleasure.

Only gentle sleep steals me.

ELEVEN

NATE

Eva's asleep on the bed and her soft breathing is the only sound I hear. After our scene, she fell asleep. The first thing I did was get her dressed, and walked out of Sins with her in my arms. I brought her back to my place because I needed to make sure she was okay after what I did.

She didn't stir. I wore her out and I knew that when she wakes up, she'd be in pain. As soon as we got home, I laid her on my bed, massaged every inch of her body, and made sure she was warm.

Agony sliced through me when I saw her look at me with both anger and lust while I fucked that blonde's mouth. I was going to eat her cunt too, but something about the way Eva looked at me stopped me from going through with it. I couldn't allow myself to see the pain on her face anymore. To recognize the image in those blue eyes of what a fucking monster I am.

Last night was the final straw. I gave her the scene I didn't plan. Her need for rough, forceful sex is clear in her eyes. When I pinned her down and choked her, she was drenched. I took advantage of the situation. I shouldn't have done it there. Not with them watching, but I couldn't stop myself.

I've always had a penchant for pain, for making women cry, and Eva cried. She fucking bawled her eyes out, screeched my name as I took her ass. Once it was over, I feared I'd hurt her, but thankfully, there wasn't blood.

Memories assault me. I wasn't sure I'd be able to get us out of there and home safely, I was shaking so much. Fury ran through my veins at the thought of me doing to Eva what I did to Emelia. Gulping the brandy down in one swallow, I allow my head to drop back against the window pane.

Tiny raindrops tap against the glass, lulling me into a false sense of security. With Eva asleep in my bed like she belongs there, like she's always been there, and me here watching over her. Like we're a normal couple. But

I know we're not, and I think she does too. When she wakes up, she'll walk out. The same way Emelia did. And I'll be left as the monster again. I know I am. Never once did I deny it.

The window seat where I'm perched offers me a view of her beautiful curves, which are covered by the comforter. She's hidden, but I know every inch of her form. I watch her peaceful breaths for a moment, just taking in the softness of the woman I'd hurt earlier.

I'm not even a week into knowing her and I'm already watching her sleep, that addiction easily glaring at me. All the things I did with Emelia, I'm doing with her. Addicted to her taste, her smile, and her fucking tears. Everything.

It feels as if I'm watching all the ways she's slowly turning me into someone I don't recognize, someone I can live with, but I've fucked it by our scene. By allowing my monster to step into the light, into her light. I can't keep her as much as I want to. I'm afraid I'll take that beautiful soul and shatter it into a million pieces. Instead of being the Dominant she needs, I'm turning into a man she's slowly falling for. I see her mind racing, her eyes holding the emotion that's so dangerous for us both. That's why I had to make sure she hates me. That when she looks at me again, she sees the dark, demented, fucked up fiend.

Guilt. Greed. Depravity.

Above all, there's one emotion I hide. My world doesn't allow for it. My desires don't include love. How can you love someone that allows you to do that to them? I thought I loved Emelia, she thought she loved me, but it wasn't love. It was lust.

Love is pure, beautiful. It's an emotion you bestow on someone you want to lift into the light. Not someone you drag into the dark with you.

I don't love Eva, not yet. It's too soon, but I know that if she were to stay with me, I'd fall. And I'd fall hard. The problem is, I'll pull her into my world and that's not where she belongs. Even though her tastes are more volatile, she needs someone who can mend her, who can make her whole. I'm not him. I can never be that man for her.

Thoughts tumble through my mind. My fear of allowing someone to love me coils like a serpent waiting to attack and the poison it holds keeps me up late into the night. Most times I'll sit here and watch the sun rise. I'll see the light break through the dark and finally feel at ease. How is it a grown man is afraid of the dark?

Darkness. It's where my secrets hide. It's where my desires were born. And there's no place for love.

"Nate?" Her voice startles me, her gaze lands on me in the dark. Even though she can just about make out my form in the room, she seeks me like a beacon. I can't deny the tether between us, it's real. Too fucking real.

"I'm here, sweetheart," I assure her, pushing to my feet. I make my way to the bed while her eyes take me in. As soon as I slip under the covers, I pull her against me. Her soft sigh is the only thing that eases the ache in my chest at what I'm going to have to do. It feels as if I'm losing my mind. Perhaps I am. One part of me tells me to let her go, the other begs me to keep her.

Moments later, she's asleep in my arms. Her body cocooned by mine. Held tight. Kept safe. Only hours to go before she walks out of my home and I'll need to say goodbye. She may have agreed to the contract, the three weeks, but I can't do this to her again. I can't allow myself to hurt the woman that I'm holding as if she's my lifeline. I'd rather sink into the darkest, murkiest depths.

In the dark, I find solace with her in my arms. I revel in the few moments I have with the woman that's stealing pieces of me, holding them fast in her grip.

As I watch her sleep, a memory of the day I lost Emelia steals me.

It's early morning, that much I know from the sun just peeking through the window. The shuffling of material woke me. When I roll over, I find Emelia getting dressed, her body moving slowly, and then she turns to me. Our eyes lock. Mine fall to her neck, taking in the blue and purple finger marks that I left last night.

"I'm leaving, Nate. I can't be what you need," she says sadly. The words jolt me into action, and I'm out of the bed in seconds. As soon as I get close to her she steps away, fear paints her expression. "Don't."

"Melly, please?"

"It's the last time, Nathan, we're two very different people, needing very different things. I may enjoy kinky, but…" she sighs, the agony clear in her voice.

"Look at me," I order.

She lifts her chin, giving me a view of her bruised neck. I did that. The monster that I can no longer hide in the dark hurt her and now she's leaving.

Anguish, as if I'm being sliced open, grips my chest and I half expect blood to be dripping from the flesh. "I can change. Go for help. You said you wouldn't leave me."

"I said I'd be your slave, not your fucking punching bag!"

"I never hit you!" I bite out, anger taking precedence, my body shuddering with rage. Fear and love, lust and desire all meld together in a dangerous storm.

"No, you didn't. You hurt me in other ways, Nate. You made me love you," she says. "I fell in love with the monster, the man, and even though they're one person, I can't live with either of them. Not anymore."

"Melly, last night was..." I trail off my explanation because I don't know what to say. How to keep her. I don't know how to explain that my hunger for her takes control and I can't help myself. "You wanted it. You could've called out your safe word. You know this."

"Yes," she sighs, dropping her gaze to the floor. "I just wanted to trust you wouldn't go too far. I did trust you. I'm *just not made for this… And… I love you, Nathan, but I can't give you the dark you desire so much."*

"I told you I can't love. I've never been able to feel anything other than what we have." When I try to take a step closer to her she once again moves away, holding up her hand to stop me in my tracks. Her body shivers, her eyes are glossed over with tears which turns my blood cold with frustration.

"I've called a cab. Don't call me. Just… don't come near me again." Her voice is filled with resignation. It's over and it's all my fault. My inability to love, to give her affection has ripped her from me.

"Melly, I can't lose you." The rasp in my tone drips with loss. As if part of me is being torn violently and I'm useless to stop it.

"Why? Why Nathan? Tell me you love me!" Anger dances in her eyes. Like the sun rising behind us, shedding light on our relationship, I see her, I see the tears I've caused. And I can't answer her. I can't tell her I love her because I'm not built that way. Love isn't something I can feel. Yes, I care for her, I want her. Owning her is all I can do, and I know that's not what she needs.

"I can't."

"Bullshit, Nathan! You refuse to even allow it near you. That's exactly why I'm leaving. You allow your monster to rule your fucking life, Nathan. You are capable of so much, you can love! But you know what, you don't want to. That's your problem. And you know why?" She doesn't wait for me to answer, instead, she finally touches me by prodding my chest, shoving me backward and I can't do anything to respond because I'm in shock at her fire. "Because you're a fucking monster! You love hurting me! You get hard when you see me cry! Who does that? Only a vile fucking monster!"

The word rings in my head, I know I am. I know it's true. Can I love? If I allow myself to feel, could I ever love Emelia? No. I know I can't. I've never been able to.

Her eyes drop to my hands which fist at my sides and a smirk, both angry and amused, curls her lips. She nods with knowing. Understanding paints her beautiful face, her eyes no longer glimmer with sadness, but pity.

"You knew who I was and what you were getting into, Melly. This," I gesture between us with my index finger. "It's something you walked into eyes wide fucking open. You saw my monster and you still loved me." I hiss in frustration. If she thinks I'll fall to my knees for a woman, she's sorely mistaken.

I may care for her, maybe even love her, but I will not be topped from the bottom.

"Goodbye, Nathan Ashcroft. I hope you burn in hell." Her words are venom seeping into my veins. I want to hurt her right now. The need to bend her over, whip her with my belt is the only thing I can focus on. I can't even bring myself to hold her, to want to wrap my arms around her and keep her safe. But who am I keeping her safe from when I'm the one who hurt her?

She spins on her heel, with her purse and coat in hand, I watch her walk out the door, slamming it and I'm left alone. Shutting my eyes, I allow the pain and agony to take hold. I don't cry. I don't feel sadness, I feel anger.

Tonight, I'll walk into Sins and I'll find a willing slut to take my punishment. And when I do it, I'll picture her in all her naked glory. Those incredible curves, that long chocolate hair, and those eyes. Piercing, judging, pitying. Some pain slut will pay tonight.

TWELVE

EVA

Warmth cocoons me, but as soon as I roll over, pain jolts me upright. "Oh god," I groan.

Hands, strong and gentle, stroke my back, my skin tingling from the sensation. When he touches me, it feels as if he's a balm to my wounds. A healing force to the pain I once endured. Men are dangerous creatures. They're also animals when it comes to hurting and healing, they'll easily break someone, but putting that person back together is not in their forte.

After everything we went through last night, I should walk out immediately. Perhaps he thinks that too, but I can't. There's no way I can leave him. We both broke last night. We were two damaged souls coming together and with our fragmented pieces, they fit perfectly. It was as if both dark, shimmering parts had always been the missing portion of the other, creating an artwork fit for hell.

"Sweetheart," he says. His voice is tentative, and I know why.

That same voice which gave me pain, pleasure, and surety last night, calms me in the bright light of day. Physical pain is easier to understand than emotional, it's easier to come to terms with. Last night, it wasn't what he'd done that changed us, or me, it was the way he cared for me after.

The tenderness he touched me with, and the affectionate words weren't that of a monster. As much as he believes he is, I don't see him as one. I see him as a man so deeply in need of love, that I already find myself falling. Can you love someone in such a short time? Is that even possible?

"What's the time?" I ask, shifting onto my sore ass, attempting not to wince as I roll over. "Shit, that seriously stings," I say, glancing up into his regretful eyes. "Nate?" I murmur, frowning.

"I'm sorry," he says, breaking eye contact and shifting off the bed. He leaves me cold and lonely. His body is rigid. His eyes are swollen and the dark circles that surround them make those deep brown orbs black. It's clear he didn't sleep last night.

"For what?" I push off the bed slowly. My body aches and creaks as I move, but in the pain, I easily recall the pleasure he gave me. No man has ever been able to wipe away my fears the way he has. Since *that* night, when I went to a stranger for what I needed, no other man, not even Carrick, could bestow the darkened, sick desire I have for it, for breath play, for forced role play, for the things most women shy away from.

All my life I thought I was sick for wanting it. I thought I'd been broken by a man I trusted. Even when I let Carrick take my virginity, he couldn't wash away the pain and agony of what had happened to me.

"I've called you a cab, it will be here in an hour. You need to eat and—"

"Wait!" Stalking over to Nate, I grip his arm, turning him to face me. "You're sending me away?" I demand, anger slowly heating my skin, turning me livid with rage. "What the fuck, Nathan? You can't do what you did last night and expect me to walk out of here. Am I not meant to choose? The contract still stands. Unless you want me gone. Was last night a *fuck you goodbye?*" I'm screeching by the time I finish my tirade, but he just watches me. Doesn't move.

"I can't be with you, Eva. I'm a monster. I'll hurt you."

Without thinking, I rear back, finding his cheek with my hand. I feel the sting as soon as I hear the sound. My palm smarts with the force of the harsh slap I've just delivered. "Fuck you!" Storming by him, I don't make it very far when he's on me. His body, so much larger than mine, tackles me to the soft red carpet. I grip the wool below my fingers, trying to drag myself from his vice grip, but I can't. His hand is in my hair. His hips pin me to the floor.

"Eva, calm the fuck down," he growls in my ear, but I don't see past the anger and heartache he's just caused. I can't see him because my monster has come out to play, and she's not happy. The mirror reflects us in an image of vileness. My head is tugged back; we stare each other down in the glass. "Look at that! Look! You see us? We're fucked up, Eva." He grunts forcefully in my ear, his lips on the smooth shell causing me to shudder with need that's coiling low in my gut. "You need someone who'll calm your storm."

"I need someone who's going to dance in my fucking hurricane and not run from it. If you're such a fucking coward, then leave me alone. I'll find another man who isn't afraid." My words are hateful, spitting venom where I know he's hurting. We're dangerous together, a force of nature that could most probably kill the other, but I know without him, I'll be lost. "I'll find a Master who'll give me what I need if you're so scared to give me you," I spit angrily. I'm taunting him. Provoking him to do what I need. My words slam into him because when I look in the mirror again, his gaze has darkened.

Black.

Sinful, depraved, and filthy.

"I'm a fucking coward, am I?" he grunts, pressing his hips against my ass, which is still hurting from what he did to me last night, but I find myself squeezing my thighs, my body reacting, responding to the need for more. I crave the violence, I ache for it.

"Let me go, Nate," I order, but it's no use. He's too far gone. He shoves my panties down. His fingers find my core easily. He knows my body better than I do. A smirk curls his lips when he probes my already wet hole.

"Seems like my sweet slut wants to play," he says, his face grinning manically in the mirror. I raise my hips in response.

Yes, I do want to play. I want him. I need him. He's the only one who understands my need.

"I want you, Nathan. I'll sign the contract," I manage to utter, stilling him immediately. His fingers inside my core, his hand fisting my long dark hair, his eyes boring into me. Piercing me with questions, confusion, and agony.

Before I have time to fathom what's happening, he shifts off me, the heat of his body leaving me as he moves away. I've never seen a man so feral and so scared at the same time. Like an animal that's been wounded, he scurries back on his ass, his cock hard, jutting out from his boxers. I'm on my knees, crawling toward him.

"Leave. Get out. I want you to go," he commands.

"What?" I glare, shooting daggers from my eyes, hoping to kill him with a look. The room darkens like the stormy sky before a thunderstorm. It swirls around us as I move closer to him.

"Get the fuck out!" His voice booms around me, and I blink, my mind blank of responses because shock has stolen words from my brain. He doesn't move and stupidly, I decide to go to him. I shouldn't, his mood tells me to obey, but my heart, that fragile damaged muscle, tells me otherwise. I move toward him, my hand out in surrender.

"I'm not leaving you," I tell him firmly, not wavering in my response, no confusion in my voice. He looks up, his eyes trained on mine. When my hand touches his leg, he seems to flip from the enraged monster to a man and I see him.

He reminds me of the story of Jekyll and Hyde. Before my very eyes, as if a switch is flipped on and off, the man himself turns from one to the other. Monster and man. He's fighting the dark with everything inside, but it taunts his soul as it slowly eats away at him.

"You should," he sighs, finality in his tone. The sadness that now hangs around us is stifling. I need to do something to force it away.

Shaking my head, I manage to wiggle my way

onto his lap, tugging the boxers down freeing his shaft. As soon as I straddle him, I feel the heat of his cock at my wet pussy. I don't give him time to object, reaching between us, I grip his shaft, and slowly sink down onto him until he's balls deep inside me. We're connected. There's nothing that can break this tether.

My hands find purchase on his shoulders. The tension eases at my touch, and I watch his head drop back in pleasure when I move. Allowing my hips to rock back and forth, moving slowly, gently at first, but when his hands grip my body, he moves me faster.

"Fuck me, sweet slut. Ride my cock," he utters with his eyes shut so tight as if he's in pain if I don't, but in agony if I do. "Use me for your pleasure, I need you," his words tumble between us, hanging in the air like promises, threats, and dangerous vows.

He lifts his head, opening his eyes, and watches me. Sweet and slow has never been my thing, I've never let it affect me. When I've been fucked, it's been deep and hard, fast and brutal, but this is something else. Even though I'm on top, riding him, he's very much in control. It's not the angry fuck we had last night, or almost did moments ago, this is filled with affection.

His fingers stroke the skin on my hips, circling the smoothness, teasing and taunting me. I lock my eyes on his heated gaze. It's electric, shooting currents through my veins, and every inch of my skin erupts in goose bumps. We may fight this, we may convince ourselves that it's best if we part ways, but deep down we both know it's a lie.

"I need you, Nate. Don't push me away," I tell him, emotion cracking in my voice. My throat raw from last night's begging and pleading, with the tears I shed in pain and pleasure. His hands move over the globes of my ass, gripping the flesh painfully, opening me up, and I know he's looking at me in the mirror. Watching me move above him, taking my pleasure along with his in a slow and gentle fuck. It heats my blood, sizzling through me, alighting my core with a blaze, along with my heart.

My thumb is positioned on his neck and I can feel his pulse, it's skittering in his neck. I watch his throat work as he swallows. He knows as much as I do, this is it. There's so much more between us than two people enjoying carnal pleasure.

"You're so beautiful. Every inch of you. I want to own all of you, Eva." His fingers tease my puckered hole, it's sensitive from his brutal fucking last night, but the way he's stroking it so gently causes my pussy to clamp down on his cock. "Yes, that's it. Come for me, sweetheart." Tenderness laces his words, sending me over the edge as I find release. It's the most incredible feeling, tightening my belly, my core pulsing around his rigid hardness. His fingers teasing me.

My body wracks with an orgasm and as the tears fall, I revel in the saltiness that reach my lips. A waterfall of emotion erupts from me along with a release so heartfelt I'm left breathless, my fingers digging into his skin as if I'm trying to draw blood.

As I come down from my high, I watch him through the blur of emotion that's broken forth. His lips quirk into a sad smile which causes my heart to ache. It feels as if I've known him all my life. And just the thought of him wanting me gone grips me painfully, leaving me an utter mess.

With care, he lifts me off his cock, and I don't ignore the fact that he didn't come. "Is everything okay?" I ask as he pushes off the floor. Offering me a hand, he tugs me up, pulling me into a tight hold. He doesn't answer me and something inside me aches. Something's wrong. So very fucking wrong.

"Eva, I need you to make sure that this is what you want. Don't sign the contract because I asked you to. All of what happened last night, that's something I need. I promise you, sweet girl, one day I'll hurt you. One day the monster you so actively seek will shatter you one final time. I don't want you to go, but I don't want you to stay either. This has to be up to you."

"I'm a big girl, I can make my own decisions. And I'm not scared of you, Nate." My words cause him to flinch, but he doesn't respond. Instead he turns away and I miss his eyes on me. The way he runs his fingers through his hair tells me there's so much more he's hiding. More to the elusive man I find myself intoxicated by. Drunk on want. High on desire. And craving my next fix.

"Then you'll find the paperwork in the living room. I've set out a pen, sign it. Once that's done, we'll go for lunch." He leaves me gaping at his retreating form. I move around the room, finding my discarded clothes, and quickly pulling them on.

As I step into the living room, I find the contract like he said on the table. My phone beside it buzzes with a message. When I swipe my finger over the screen, I read the message slowly. Word for word, my blood runs cold. They've found me.

I thought I could escape. I thought if I ran far enough, kept a low profile, she'd let me live my life. But that's what happens when you allow yourself a false sense of security. Picking up the contract, I stare at it, wondering if this is a good idea. Not because I shouldn't sign it, but because I don't want Nathan to be dragged into the shit my life has always been. I don't want her to know about him. And right now, she won't give up until she's run me out of town.

Life is full of choices. And this is my fork in the road. I should walk away. But I'm selfish, I'm greedy for everything he offers. So, I pick up the pen and sign my name on the thick black line.

I'm now owned by Nathan Ashcroft.

THIRTEEN

NATE

One week later

My phone buzzes again. I know who it is. Even though I should, I don't look at the screen, I don't want to respond. I've kept her at bay with lies that I'd let Eva go, keeping our relationship a secret. I should've known that secrets will eventually come to light.

Even though she signed the contract, I've still not told her the truth. The reason I'd found her two weeks ago. It's been fourteen days of bliss with her. I've never been in love, but I can tell there's something different about what I have with the raven-haired beauty. She's given me everything—her mind, her body, and her soul. But she's holding back. There are still secrets she hides and I have a feeling I know exactly what they involve.

Her heart is still hidden, it's locked away and each night we bare ourselves to each other, I know she hasn't yet allowed me into that one place that she's kept locked up tight. I've given her my heart. I've placed it in her hands without regret.

The phone buzzes again. It's been ringing off the hook, I've ignored it all morning and I know deep down the more I do, the deeper the hole that's going to swallow me gets. I shouldn't have taken her, pursued her. But once again, my selfish nature, my addiction to beautiful women, to Eva specifically, has slowly eaten away at my resolve and I couldn't help myself. I'd convinced myself that we could work.

I should have known it wouldn't last. My happiness is not warranted. A monster doesn't deserve love. I should be burned at the stake. The threat that hangs over my head is one I can no longer ignore.

As I make my way to the front door of my apartment, I know my sweet slut is nowhere to be seen this morning because she hates me right now. Her ass is sore, her pussy is raw from the way I used her last night. When I got the call to my office number yesterday evening, I was livid.

I'd come home in a mood which was filled with

anger. Not at Eva, at myself. I did this. After I'd taken my sweet slave into my dungeon, I wasn't myself. I'd been caught up in my dark thoughts and when I finally snapped out of it, when I saw what I'd done, I realized it's time to walk away.

When I first met the delicate Eva, I was enamored. Now, I know I've fucked up. I've done the one thing I didn't want to do—let my heart into the equation. "I'm leaving," I call out to nobody. I know she's not coming to kiss me goodbye. She shouldn't. If her body were close to me right now I'd hurt her again. Not just physically, I'd shatter her heart. And not because I want to hurt her, but because I want to hurt myself. I don't know how to deal with the pain that comes with thoughts of losing her.

As much as I don't blame her hiding, it angers me that I've turned into the monster that I vowed never to become with her. As I walk down to my Aston Martin, in my mind I plan the things I want to do to her one last time. Pulling my phone from my pocket, I tap out a message.

Me: I suggest you meet me at Sins tonight, if you're not there on the floor naked when I walk into room one I'll make sure you can't sit for a month.

Tonight will be the end, I'll finally tell her goodbye. I'll give her one last scene. One that she craves and needs. Then, I'll send her back to Carrick. The thought of knowing she'll be in his arms before the night is over only serves to rip my dead heart from my chest. Jealousy for my friend is unwarranted, but I feel it nonetheless. It doesn't matter who it is, the man who finally gets her will forever be on my shit list.

Slipping into the driver's seat, I settle back and sigh with resignation. That's why in this lifestyle, or this world, there's no room for love. Once you fall in love with a Dominant or submissive, you're fucked. It's a harsh lifestyle. Kinks that hurt, needs that break, and desires that can set off any amount of emotion.

All the years I've practiced I've never allowed myself to care for a woman more than the one night of aftercare, especially after Emelia. As soon as they walk out of the room, I forget them. Their name is not important, neither are their hopes and dreams. The only thing that matters is the hole I use, cunt or ass, or even mouth. Other than that, I don't need more.

That was before this. Before Eva and the agreement that changed my life.

Before I start the engine, my phone buzzes.

Sweet Slut: As you please, Sir Nate.

Her words only serve to heat my blood as I head down the driveway and out onto the road toward my office. There's never been a time I wasn't in control. Eva fucks with that. She makes me forget I'm in charge. But I know I'm only kidding myself because as much as I want to own her, she owns me just as much.

When I reach the office, I park in my designated spot and head up to the top floor. Our firm is one of the best. Spending five years building a reputation as the top accountancy firm in the city wasn't an easy feat, but my partner, Asher Briggs and I, have set ourselves up with a name brand that is not overlooked. A&B Finance has been in the Financial Times with more accolades than

I can count. Our clients know we're the only name in finance. If you need advice, representation, or anything in between, we know how to deal with it.

Asher has known me since college. We met while studying for our Degree's and spent most of our time learning about the BDSM community together. Our friendship grew from strength to strength. His penchant differs from mine considerably. More of a sweet, loving Dominant, he's caring and romantic, whereas I love to see tears.

When he told me he was going to join me at Sins a few months ago, I was over the moon. He's still not found a submissive yet, but I know with his good looks and his calm nature, he'll easily snag a beauty. He's a huge fan of women bound in leather and lace. I've seen his collection of blindfolds made of the material. Exquisite.

I make my way into the reception area of our floor, finding it quiet for this early in the morning. Most of the staff are normally milling around, chattering with a cup of coffee, however, this morning seems to be calmer.

"Good morning, Sir," the soft tone of Belinda comes from my left as I pass by her desk. Our receptionist, a beautiful blonde, smiles at me demurely. I could easily have her swallowing my dick, but she's staff. That's one thing I never do is fuck my employees.

"Belinda, I hope you're well today," I smile, offering her a nod.

She blushes beautifully. Submissive. "I am. Thank you, Sir." Her voice is delicate, like the finest silk, but there's no comparison to my Eva. I head through the main doors without another glance at her and find Asher talking to his personal assistant.

"Hey, Nate," he greets, dropping the folder on her desk and turning to me with a smirk. He offers a hand in greeting which I accept and shake.

"Ash," I acknowledge him, and then offer the beauty sitting behind her desk a smile before making my way to my office. The open plan space is sparsely furnished with a beautiful ornate dark oak desk which takes up almost half the office as my throne, with a faux leather office chair behind it. When we purchased the rental agreement, I sought this office before anyone else could. Mainly because I have a view that's worth more money than I can count.

My desk overlooks a city that I can't help admiring every day. There are bookshelves that cover the wall to my left in the same dark wood as the desk. In the center, I have a black leather sofa and small coffee table made of glass and steel. It's not modern, but it had some beautiful touches that fit my personality to the T. On the right is a wall of glass overlooking Chicago.

When I step further into the space, I know I'm about to get the third degree. I've been talking to Asher, getting advice on how to handle my feelings with Eva. Not knowing how to tell someone you love them isn't easy. Especially when you're not meant to have these feelings for them. When your agreement is exactly that, a business arrangement.

"How is Eva?" Asher questions, following me into my office and shutting the door behind him.

"Fine." My answer is clipped and his chuckle is the response I knew I'd get. He knows how I am with women—a cold, heartless bastard. But what he doesn't know is that I have to leave her for reasons that I can't even explain. I can't tell her why. I definitely can't tell her the truth.

"Did you two have a fight again?" He smirks. I meet his intense gaze and nod. "Jesus, Nate. You've got a beautiful woman who will do anything for you and you are fucking it up," he admonishes me with a frustrated lilt to his tone. He's one of two people who can talk to me like that without repercussions, the other being Carrick Anderson. Also, he's right.

"She loves me. She hasn't said it in so many words, but I can see it in her eyes." I sigh, settling on the chair and watching his reaction.

His shocked gaze snaps to me. "And you didn't tell her you love her? I know you do." His question is filled with incredulity, his statement heated with confidence.

"Why would I?" Truth is, I wanted to tell her that last night, I also wanted to ask her to stay, and that's where the problem lies.

"You don't love her?" he questions warily, folding his arms across his chest. I don't respond. I can't. Because it would be a lie. "Jesus, Nate. You are going to lose the best thing that's ever happened to you because you're acting like a stubborn child."

Rising from my chair, I pin him with a glare. "Are

you sure you want to talk to me like that?"

"What are you going to do? Whip me? I'm not one of your slaves, Nate. And yes, I'll speak to you any way I want to."

"Asher, when you find a slave, submissive, whatever, and you see her look at you with those adoring eyes ready to love you even in your darkest state, and you have all that in danger, then you'll know how it feels." I shouldn't have said anything, but I need his advice. Even though I can't tell him the whole truth, maybe I can let him in on what's going on. Maybe he can help me.

"What do you mean?"

"I don't have a choice in the matter." I look up, wondering if this is such a good idea. Maybe he'll drop it, but if I know Asher Briggs, he doesn't take anything at face value. And he's known me too long to walk away from what I've just told him.

"You're going to lose a woman you love over some... what?"

"Nothing. Eva doesn't understand my needs anymore." The lie weighs on my tongue like a lead weight. I don't meet his gaze when I spew out another.

"I can't be with one woman." I sigh, dropping back in my chair, spinning it around so I don't have to face his judgmental glare.

"What are you talking about? You love her! That means more than—"

"Jesus, Asher! It's not her. Okay?" I grunt in frustration. He's going to drag this out of me until I'm coming clean, until he's found out why I'm really walking away.

"What?" He asks, shock lacing his tone. "Nathan, if there's something going on here. If you're in trouble of any kind, I need to know. Not because of the company, but because you're a friend."

"There's something that I haven't told you," I face him once more. "I'm being blackmailed. I need to let her go. It's the only way I know she's safe. It's the only way I know she'll leave with her heart safe and me out of her life. I'm the fucking monster and I've almost broken her completely. If she finds out what I've done…" My confession doesn't give away my secret, but it allows me some sort of understanding from my best friend. At least, I hope it does.

"Nate, are you still blaming yourself over Emelia? Are you always going to allow yourself to be dragged down by one fucking mistake? I told you a long time ago, when she first left you, that doesn't make you a monster. If it did, half of the Dominants and Master's in Sins would have their slaves walking out. We all have our own kinks. Some darker than others. You can't blame yourself for what Emelia couldn't handle."

"It wasn't that. It was the fact that Emelia loved me and I couldn't love her."

He watches me for a moment before rising from the chair. Placing both palms flat on my desk, he leans in. "Look me in the eye and tell me you do not love Eva. Tell me without flinching, without fucking blinking and then I'll believe you." He waits. We're at an impasse because he knows I can't. Silence is our friend, it sits between us waiting for the moment I finally admit that I can love. That I'm capable of feeling something other than guilt, regret and hate. "I thought so."

When I glance at his darkened eyes, I can read the frustration on his face. It's eating away at him and me. There's nothing more I can say to strengthen my case to leave, unless I tell him the whole truth and I can't do that. Shame squeezes my chest at what I did, but I'll make it right. I have to.

"Nate—"

"Enough, Asher! It's done. I can't give Eva what she wants. Tonight, she'll need to say goodbye." Shuffling the pages on my desk, I attempt to look busy, but deep down, my body is trembling with anger, fear, and frustration.

"You're making a mistake, Nate. That's all I'm saying." He turns to walk out of my office, leaving me in a maelstrom of emotion that's too much for me to handle. I can't deal with this shit right now.

Pulling my phone from my jacket pocket, I tap out a response to my pet.

Me: I want you wearing that red dress. No panties. Make sure you've got your pretty pink butt plug in. Tonight will be painful.

Her response is immediate and I picture her lying on my bed waiting for my messages. She spends her days at home, and works most nights at Sins. When I walk into the house after a long day at the office, she's the first thing I see. It's heaven. A perfect life that can never be.

Sweet Slut: I thought you wanted me naked?

Chuckling, I tap out my response. Her sassiness is one of the many things I love about her. One on a long list of traits that make me want to keep her safe, hold her in my arms and tell her everything will be okay even when I don't believe it myself.

Me: Don't be sassy. I'm in a bad mood, and I don't need your smart mouth.

Sweet Slut: Perhaps you should punish me, Sir.

Me: Don't doubt that you'll be in pain tonight, Sweet Slut. I'll make sure your ass is bright red, your cunt will be raw when I'm done fucking you. And make no mistake, if you touch your sweet hole right now, I'll know. You are not to come today. Meet me at six.

As soon as I hit send, I shove my phone in the drawer. I know if we keep this up I'll be in my car heading home to fuck her hard. I have a meeting in fifteen minutes, I need to focus on work. Inhaling a deep breath, I calm myself and open my laptop and go through the figures for my client. Even though I'm staring at spreadsheets, my mind is on one woman and I know that I'm in too deep.

As much as I want to deny it. I can't. I've fallen in love with her. And even though I don't want to, I know I'm going to have to let her go. Tonight, we will play our final scene together and when all's said and done, we will say goodbye for the last time. I'll have to walk away from the only woman I ever wanted and needed more than a submissive, more than a slave. The thought sends me spiraling into the dark abyss I've lived in all my life and I focus on the only constant I have. Work.

I should have let her go after that first night in my playroom, I should've walked away, but I lied and as time passed, it only built into something more. My own addictions to money, gambling, and my greed has put me here, and there's no other way out.

FOURTEEN

EVA

I read the messages and reread them. Over and over until they're blurry to my teary gaze. I want things to be different. I thought they would be when I finally signed the contract. He's kept me safe. I haven't heard from my mother again, but deep down I know I'll never be rid of them until I see her and that vile excuse for a boyfriend behind bars or dead.

I wanted to tell Nate last night. To come clean. To finally admit all the shit I'd been hiding. But I also wanted to tell him those three damning words. And in that moment, I ached to hear them from his lips as well. For him to reciprocate and tell me he loves me too, but I couldn't and he didn't.

Instead, I kept quiet, and he whipped me. He made me scream, cry, and then he cared for me. Showed me affection which didn't have the normal effect of soothing the emotion.

Aftercare means you feel safe, cocooned in your dominant's arms. Instead, my heart hurt more than ever before because I knew then that I'll never have the one thing I want from him. Love. I can't be too angry with him though, I've not yet given him my heart, my truth. I thought we'd be able to overcome that, to both be able to allow ourselves to feel.

He may give his body freely, not only to me, but to the other slaves he's been with in the past, and that should've been a sign. A big fucking neon flashing sign to tell me to steer clear. But I wouldn't have listened. I never do.

Now, as I lie on his bed, dressed in the soft, fluffy bathrobe he bought me, I know it will be the last time I'm in his home. The shower I had earlier was warm, calming my warring mind, but as the seconds tick by and the time he said to meet nears, anxiety attacks me again.

I've always trusted my intuition. It's been spot on all my life. When something bad is about to happen, I feel it, like a thunderstorm in the sky, I see it coming. Only this time I didn't get out of the way. I walked straight into the eye of it and now I'm caught in its clutches, spinning out of control.

Last night when he arrived home from work he was cold. Closed off in a way I hadn't seen him in our time together. It's going into the third week of our relationship, I know him, I know his moods. And this tells me there's trouble ahead. Only, I have no way of knowing what it is or even why.

I normally spend my days reading, studying, but today I find my heart heavy. Even the temptation to taunt him by telling him I'm touching myself hasn't given me the thrill it normally does.

Yes, I enjoy the punishments, and I tend to tease him because it's our game. But I feel as if something's about to crack in the fragile world we've built together. I'm not stupid. I know that his work is important to him, but when he got home last night, something in his demeanor shifted. There's something he's hiding from me and I think he'd rather let me go than let me in.

Over the time we've spent together, I've been his. I've given him me completely. But he's always held back.

I made the mistake of loving him. I fell, hard and fast. I knew I shouldn't but the heart wants what it shouldn't. I couldn't stop it happening.

Every time I recall our first time, when he fucked me in front of others, when he used me like a toy, I wonder if he somehow chose me because I was special. Then I'm slammed back to the present and I know if I were he'd wouldn't be planning to release me tonight. No. I'm not special. I've never been. I'm just a toy that offers him pleasure. I've given him everything a man could want, and now I know he's about to return me without so much as a second glance.

Pain grips my heart. I'm not ready to say goodbye. I slip on the heels he bought me last weekend when we went shopping. The sleek silver sandals glisten under the low lights. Red and silver. His favorite colors.

My long dark hair hangs down my back in waves. My blue eyes are bright with unshed tears, but I can't do anything about that. I know the end is coming and as much as I want him to love me, I know a man like him isn't capable of love. He's not going to give me forever.

I knew this when I submitted to him. I blame myself.

My phone vibrates on the dressing table alerting me to a message from him no doubt.

When I swipe my finger over the screen I find his name glowing brightly at me.

Sir: I'm leaving work now. I trust you'll be on time. I'm not in the mood for waiting tonight.

Sighing, I tap out my response and hit send while I make my way to the door. He bought me a small Audi A3, cherry red, which he told me reminded him of me. Cherries. His favorite fruit. Only, as I slip into the driver's seat of my car, I know I'm no longer his first choice.

Me: In the car, Sir. I'll be there soon.

As I make my way toward Seven Sins, I feel a sense of foreboding overcome me. It hangs heavy around me like I'm driving to my end. Swallowing deeply, I turn on the radio and listen to the mixed playlist he made me when he bought the car. The song *Bad Romance* echoes through the speakers in Jared Leto's voice. He did a cover of the original and to be honest, I prefer his version because it's more haunting which fits with how I'm currently feeling.

As soon as I pull up to the club, I park and exit the vehicle with anxiety tightening my stomach. My hands tremble because I know what's going to happen when I walk in there. He's going to leave me and there's nothing I can do about it. Our three weeks are almost up. The contract will end tonight, a few days earlier than we agreed, but it was never up to me. It's final and so is our relationship.

Each step I take is like a nail in the coffin, nearing the doors, I try to put on a brave face. If Carrick sees me, he'll know something's wrong. My shoes click on the asphalt as I head toward the large black double doors.

"Ms. Gallagher," the bouncer greets with a smile as his eyes drink me in.

I can't help shuddering in frustration. There's only one man I want looking at me like that. And that is where my mistake lies. I shouldn't have fallen. I should've stayed strong.

"Hello." I smile back. He opens the door and allows

me in, but I don't miss the way he tries to glance down the front of my dress. As soon as I walk into the decadence that is Seven Sins, I feel like I'm walking backward. I'm not moving into a future with Nathan, I'm strolling back into the pain and hurt that I've been hiding from.

"Eva."

My name drags me from my inner turmoil. I turn to Dylan working the bar, he's smiling at me like he's missed me. I've known him for a long time, almost five years.

"Hey, D, can I please get a shot of tequila?" I ask, settling on the stool. When he sets the shot glass on the counter, I pick it up and down it without salt or lemon.

"Are you okay?" He frowns in concern.

I don't respond, instead, I slam the glass down, motioning for him to pour me another. Once the liquid is kissing the lip of the glass, I pick it up and down it easily.

"What did that asshole do to you?" Carrick's silky-smooth tone comes from behind me as his fingertips trail my spine. Everything about my best friend is elegant. Even while he's drenched in feral darkness, there's an alluring sensuality about him. Confidence oozes from him like a cologne.

His touch heats my flesh with tingles. It's been so long, but he still affects the girl inside me. His touch is gentle, firm, yet also tender, but I know that's not Carrick Anderson. This man is one who takes control in the harshest of ways. He loves his toys, leash, chains, and whips. He's known for being a man who enjoys control in many ways. But right now, he's emanating seductiveness that eases my heartache.

"What makes you think he did anything?" I question, schooling my features. I don't need him seeing my pain, not right now. It's his fault I got involved with Nate. No, I can't blame Carrick.

"I've known you since you were sixteen, little one. I'm not stupid. Whenever you down tequila like it's water means something has happened," he says quietly, reminding me of the time he found me in the middle of the nightclub high on something, drunk on tequila, and completely out of my element. A sixteen-year-old girl trying to act like an adult. It was also the night he saved me, walking into my life like a knight.

"Carrick, do not do this now," I plead, my gaze

meeting his icy ones.

"Why, Eva? Because you're going to fall into my bed, slip onto my hard cock which needs you?" he murmurs seductively in my ear and I'm so close to saying yes when Nate walks in. I see him just behind Carrick. Two men. Both want me more than I can fathom, but only one holds my heart. I didn't realize it until this moment. Looking at both of them, I realize I know where my love lies, and it's with Nathan Ashcroft.

"Eva." The deep voice of my Sir rumbles through me like I'm tethered to him and he's tugging me back. I'm emotionally yanked into his hold where I wish he'd keep me forever. But they're all just wishes, dreams. I've become accustomed to those being surreal, nothing in life is concrete. No one ever stays. The only constant I've ever had was Rick.

He doesn't say more, but the way he's glaring at me it's as if he's bound me to his soul. And he has. I know it and he does too. I rise, turning to face him fully. His eyes are molten as they burn a hole into me. Through me. He's angry. So am I.

"Room one. Now." Without response, I turn, casting

one last glance at Carrick and head to the room in question. I don't want to know what they're about to say to each other. Both men want me. Both men can't have me. Because my heart only belongs to one.

I slink out of my dress, folding it and setting it on the cabinet in the corner. This room, much like the other's is decked in dark shades of decadence—red, purple, and dark blue. It's filled with sensual and sinful toys, but in reality, it's for Dom's and submissives who derive pleasure from play, not for a Master who enjoys what Nate does. When the door flies open, I meet his intense heated gaze.

"Thinking about Carrick's dick inside you, sweet slut?" he grunts angrily, tugging off his tie, then flinging the navy silk causing it to land on the bed. I watch him roll up the sleeves of his crisp white dress shirt. It's still impeccable, smooth, and crease-free. He's in Dominant mode and I know there'll be no changing that now. We can't talk. In the three weeks we've known each other, it's been a mix of sweet and romantic, as well as dark and dangerous, but we've always been able to talk.

His gaze penetrates me. Boring into the very depths

of my heart, gripping it tightly in his fist as if he's about to rip it out and stomp it into the ground.

"Tell me. You and Carrick looked rather cozy at the bar a moment ago. What were you talking about?" he asks, stalking toward me. His eyes glitter with danger.

"No, Sir. I wasn't thinking about his dick inside me. As a matter of fact, I was thinking about yours filling me like you always do."

He smirks. His tongue darts out, wetting his plump lower lip then his pearly white teeth bite down on the flesh which sends a jolt of pleasured heat to my clit. "Don't fucking lie to me. Tell me, Eva. Did you ever fuck Carrick?" His question is loaded with the promise of punishment and pain. That's all Nathan knows. Tonight, he's going to rain down hell fire on me because yes, I'm about to tell him something he knew all along. There's no way that Carrick didn't tell Nate about us.

"I was young when I was with him. It's been years." I give him the only answer I can, the honest one. It has been a long time since I had sex with Carrick. When he told me that he didn't think we should be together, I moved on. He still watched over me, protecting me, but there wasn't anything sexual between us. We do flirt, that's a given, but it's never been more than that. When he rounds me, gripping my chin, he gets in my face. His gaze is fire. His touch is pure anger.

"And if I didn't walk in tonight? Would you have fucked him?" he hisses in my face with rage simmering below the surface and I have a feeling it's about to erupt. The fog of need that surrounds him, clouds around me, pulling me into its thick haze and I'm caught in it, never wanting to leave. I love the dangerous Nathan as much as I do the romantic one.

"Why? Are you going to punish me if I did?" My retort is going to earn me a lashing, I have no doubt, but the way he acts when we're in certain scenes, like I no longer matter to him makes me angry. I love this man who's trying to hurt me and I know tonight is our last night together, it's written all over his face. I see it clear as day. He's saying goodbye in his own brutal way.

He's going to give me one last memory.

Pain.

Punishment.

Pleasure.

"Do not fucking test me, slut," he grunts, hisses, spits at me like I'm nothing. His nickname for me forgetting the important ingredient. It's no longer said with reverence. It's said in anger. It all becomes clear then. I know how he's kept from loving his other submissives. He pushes them away in anger. His kink of degrading them, works in his favor to keep emotion from his scenes and from his life.

I'm not them though, I'm different. There is no way I'll allow him to do this and walk away. I've seen him love. I've felt him love. And as he grips my hair, tugging my head back, my heart aches, it physically hurts for him.

"Eva, tonight I have no time for games. We'll play our scene. I felt like it needed to be in the place where we first met. Where we initially started all this..." He gestures with his hand, releasing my hair, but holding onto my arm.

Shoving him away, I step back, needing space, needing a moment to breathe through the emotion that's got a hold of my throat. It's squeezing the very breath from my lungs, and as they empty, the sting of my tears burn my eyes. His gaze is all-consuming, an inferno that's going to take me alive. Even my name on his lips sounds different. Strange even.

"I know why you brought me here." I tell him, then turn away, not wanting to look him in the eyes. I don't want to see how little I meant to him. The tender moments play in my mind. All those brutal scenes, the times I felt like I would explode from pleasure. Everything tumbles through me. All that time we spent together, each moment, every smile, laugh, and touch. The nights he slept with his cock buried inside me, connected. It's all come down to a fucking scene in a club where he's probably fucked countless others. All this time I've spent with a man who didn't even care.

"You have no fucking idea, get on your knees." His face is contorted in anger when I glance his way. I'm naked. Not because I'm not wearing clothes, but because I've bared my soul to him and now I have nothing left. He's got all of me and he's about to crush it like it means nothing.

"Why?"

"I told you once, Eva. I will make you kneel. Do it.

Kneel."

I want to fight. I want to claw his eyes out. I want to rip through his shirt, the flesh of his chest. I want to shove my hand in and find his dead, un-beating heart, and I want to tear it from his ribcage and squeeze until there's nothing left. Because that's what he's doing to me right now. That's how he's breaking me. His only slave. The only one who wanted to stay. Even after she saw the monster.

I don't respond to him with words. I merely show him with my body how I feel. All my anger dissipates into nothing and I drop to my knees, obeying the last few commands he offers. Not showing him how my heart fractures, inch by soul destroying inch.

FIFTEEN

NATE

I watch her kneel. I feel her pain right to my very fucking core. But there's nothing I can do about it. In this world, there's no room for love. There's no place for emotion. To keep her safe, I have to let her go. I've made the decision to hurt her tonight. Not in the way she expects. She wants a whipping, she needs the physical pain because she knows she'll receive the emotional pleasure. But tonight, I have to steel myself and break her emotionally.

I've come to the conclusion that love is not in the cards for me. Even though each time she obeys, every time I see her relinquish her control, offering me her supple body like it's a gift, I know that I'm not good enough for her. *Fuck*. Perhaps Carrick is better for her than I can ever be.

He's an asshole at the best of times, but deep down,

I know he's a good guy and he'll care for her. With my past coming back to haunt me the way it has, I can't risk her being hurt, so I have to walk away. I don't want her to remember me. I want her to hurt so badly tonight that she'll walk away with hate in her heart for me.

"Are you ready to play, slut?" I grunt, not using her pet name, making her feel used like all the other women I've walked into this room with. I couldn't do it at home, I needed somewhere neutral. A place where she will have someone to watch her when I walk out. Carrick and Asher know what I have planned. They both told me I'm making a mistake. And as much as I want to believe them, I don't.

"Yes, Sir," she murmurs beautifully, but doesn't look at me, her eyes are downcast, yet I notice the glistening on her lashes. Tears.

I walk to the door, pulling it open and gesturing for the blonde to come inside. I hate blondes. They do nothing for me, and that's why I've chosen her. She's perfect for what I have to do. "Eva, look at me," I command, tugging the toy I've brought into the room with us over to where my girl is kneeling. Her big blue eyes widen further when she sees the other woman. "This is Leonie, she's a toy just like you," I taunt. Humiliation. Degrading Eva isn't as easy as it is for me to do to others. Because I allowed her to get into my heart. I fell for her and now I'm going to break us both in the process.

When she didn't mean anything to me but being a hole to use, I found it easy to hurt her, and then pleasure her. But this time there will be no aftercare. This time, she'll run to the arms of another man, and I won't be angry for her doing that. Because that's my plan.

"Are you going to be a good slut for me?" I ask her, swallowing the bile that threatens to choke me. Her eyes are glossy, but she doesn't cry. Fuck, she doesn't even flinch anymore. She's steeling herself. That's good.

"Yes, Sir."

She's always been perfect at playing my games better than I ever thought. I watch her school her features. Her transparency is clear to me the moment I look at her. I step behind the blonde, undoing her bra, allowing it to fall from her shoulders. Reaching around, I pull on her nipples, tweaking them until they're pebbled peaks. "See how well she responds, slut?" Eva's gaze is pure fury, and rage dances in the depths. Soon, she'll hate me like I need her to.

I release the girl's tits and rip her panties from her tiny hips. Gripping her ass, I squeeze, opening the cheeks to see her tiny holes. Leonie is slim, she's smaller than Eva, and I know if I fucked her I'd break her in two.

"She's got beautiful little holes for me to abuse," I taunt the woman I love. I watch her shatter in front of me. And each time I glance her way, I convince myself that it's the right thing to do. I've been greedy, needing her more than I was allowed. More than I should.

"Please, Sir," she pleads, her gaze asking more than her lips are saying. She doesn't want this. But I have to do it.

"I didn't ask you to speak. Did I?" She doesn't respond. I grip the toy's hips, leading her over to the bench that sits to the left of where I have Eva kneeling. Her body shifts on her heels uncomfortably. Once our guest is bent over, I lean in and plant kisses on her thighs. Soft, delicate pecks.

A lone tear falls from Eva's left eye, trickling its way down her cheek in sadness. I reach for the smooth cunt of Leonie, stroking it, making it wet with just the tips of my index and middle fingers. Her moans fall from her lips, needy and breathy. Pleasuring her, I slip both fingers into her sodden hole, feeling her walls pulse around my digits. Sucking me into her body, she whimpers when I crook my fingers. All the while, I watch Eva.

The pain is clear, written all over her face. Agony unlike anything I've ever seen mars her beauty. It grips my chest and breathing is difficult. My mind is in turmoil. I've never hurt before, I've never allowed myself to feel any emotion for any woman I've been with. And this is why, because the emotional pain bleeds into the physical. It grips me in an iron clad fist, ripping me to shreds. "You see, Eva. This life doesn't have love in it. Emotion only breaks you, this darkness we surround ourselves in is only made for cold, dead hearts that no longer allow love in," I inform her. Knowing how much she's hurting doesn't satisfy me. I didn't think it would. I knew this would be difficult, but I didn't realize just how much so.

"Sir," she gasps, her cheeks now tearstained.

I pull my fingers from the pussy of Leonie and bring them to my lips. "The heart is something that has to be locked away. This," I gesture around us, while cleaning my fingers of the sweet, yet musky juices. "Is the only way."

I tug Blondie back up, looking her in the eyes. "Go. Thank you for offering yourself." My command is clear. I'm done with her. Disappointment etches on her pretty young face and it's all I need to know that she wanted more. *Too bad, princess.* The asshole is back.

Once I'm alone with Eva, I tug her up by her hair, and drag her to the bed. I push her down front first. Bending her over, I watch as she trembles.

"I … I didn't mean—"

I swat her ass so hard the sting on my hand smarts painfully. Her words are halted, but her whimpers are music to my ears. "You did mean. You fucking meant it when you looked at me didn't you, I heard you murmur it. You said those three fucking words that you knew would either break us or make us," I growl angrily. "I told you, Eva. Never fall in love with me, but you did. Didn't you?" I swat her again, harder this time. "Did you see me lick those sweet juices from Leonie? That's who I am. Is that the man you want to love?" My questions are harsh, the warning tone telling her I'm no longer playing around.

"Fuck you, Nate," she grinds out through clenched teeth. Every moment I've been with her she's acted perfectly, she's played into my hands like clay. I've molded her into this. It's my fault she's breaking, and it's my fault she'll be stronger for it.

"Fuck me?" Before I have time to think about it, I see red. I see the pain between us, it's a poignant entity, a force of nature that can't be hidden. Shoving my slacks down along with my briefs, I fist my cock, slapping her ass hard, marking it with my print. Red. Beauty.

"I hate you. I fucking hate you for doing this." I believe her venom spat words. They're a poison seeping directly into my veins. They meld into my blood, killing me slowly, painfully, and I deserve it.

Her words only add fury to my already angry demeanor. This is what I wanted. I grip the globes of her pert ass and slam into her hard and deep. She cries out loud and I realize she wasn't ready for me. She's normally wet, needy, this time… This time she's really angry. Her body doesn't respond, but I don't relent. I force myself in her. A screech falls from her lips, pained and agonizing, so fucking brutal it rips my chest apart.

My anger turns to anguish. The fury turns to sadness and my black dead heart ceases to beat. My cock drives into her, I know I'm hurting her, but I don't stop. I can't. I grip her hair, pulling her back so my lips are at her ear. "Is this the man you love? The fucking monster who hurts you more than he cares for you?"

"This isn't you, Nate," she manages to choke out through the tormenting strokes of my cock in her, stealing her breath. "You want me like this? Broken and shattered?" I want to nod. I want to tell her that I want to see her in nothing but pieces for me. But I don't.

My hips slam into her ass. The sounds of flesh, sex, and violence sound around us in the darkness, in the sinful place where I first found her. "This is the end, Eva. You feel this." I drive into her, stilling myself while I'm ball's deep inside her cunt. "This is the last time we'll be connected like this."

"Fuck you, Nate. Fuck you for hurting me. But more than that," she murmurs with a resounding hatred lacing each word when I feel her arousal soak my dick.

She likes it rough. She needs it like this. Like I do. "Fuck you for making me love you." Her words are filled with yearning, agony, and frustration. Her body is locked, mine is rigid. She said it. Admitting that she does indeed love me.

Love. The one word that can make a grown man fall to his knees. It can halt armies, it can shine light on the blackest of nights. But right now, I can't let it affect me.

I don't respond. I move again, needing to finish this. To let her go. I release her hair, and in three long strokes, I feel her body pulse, tighten, and milk my dick until I'm a heaving mess. When I pull out, I step back and watch my seed slowly drip from her pink flesh. It's an erotic sight. Beautiful even.

That's it. The final time I'll see her like this. She doesn't move. She keeps her head on the mattress, and I allow my eyes to drink her in, memorizing her in this state. This shattered girl of my making. I tuck myself back into my slacks, grab my jacket and I turn to the door. With my hand on the doorknob, I breathe, it's not a sigh of relief, it's an exhale of the misery that's clouding my vision.

"Goodbye, Eva."

SIXTEEN

EVA

He left me in the room last night, alone, in tears, and in pain. Not physical, but emotional. I was more than a mess and I know I'd never been hurt like that before. Even when I was younger, when my life had changed for the worst, and I was forced by the one person I trusted to do things I wouldn't wish on my worst enemy. Nothing could have prepared me for this, for the agony of heartbreak. For the agony of having your heart and soul ripped from you in a moment of passion, and allowing the person to walk out with it.

It was the first time I'd ever felt like nothing. Like the slut he called me. As I walk into Sins today, I make my way straight to the bar. Dylan glances up, offering me a smile and I feign one back. Nobody besides Carrick knows what happened between Nate and I, and I don't intend to tell them. When I slip onto the stool, Dylan sets a shot glass down in front of me without saying a word, and beside it, he places a bottle of Gran Patron Platinum. A bottle going for almost two-hundred dollars. I grab it and pour a shot.

"I don't have money," I tell Dylan after I down the shot, wincing at the burn that follows as the liquid travels down my throat. I revel in it. The physical pain will quell the emotional shit going on in my head.

"It's on Carrick. He told me to give you the bottle and for you to meet him in his office." I should've known he'd do that. The man is a bad influence on me, he's also my best friend. Although, getting me drunk could only mean one of two things—he's either trying to ease the pain, or he's going to give me pain.

I opt for the second option because right now a good harsh spanking would work wonders. I've been numb since last night when Nathan left. Nothing's felt right. I haven't cried, I haven't even thought about being on my own. Perhaps I'm in denial. Not wanting it to be true, but deep down knowing that it's done.

Grabbing my gift, I nod and head toward the staircase that leads to the offices of Mason and Carrick. The two owners of Seven Sins. Both handsome, both intensely charming, and both incredibly talented Dominants.

When I reach the dark wooden door, I knock once and wait.

"Come in," his seductive tone comes from the other side a moment later. Pushing open the door, I step into the inner sanctum of sex and shut the door behind me. Carrick's office is his playroom. With toys adorning one wall along with a dresser which hides his kinkier gems. There's also a spanking bench in the corner which I'm sure has seen many beautiful women bound to it. A large mahogany desk faces the club downstairs, through the wall of two-sided glass. There's a bar just across from where he's seated with a selection of the finest wines, brandies, and whiskies. The dim lighting and amount of leather in the room would make you think you've walked into a BDSM lair, and I suppose to Carrick it is. This is the perfect place to get lost.

"Thank you for the drink," I lift the bottle. His eyes, the color of honey, watch me, they roam over every inch of me, causing my blood to heat. The mix of alcohol and Carrick was always my downfall.

He doesn't respond, merely steeples his fingers in front of his chiseled face as he regards me with curiosity. The smooth tanned skin of his face and hands match that of his hairless sculpted chest. His tattoos are hidden by a white designer button up shirt. Dark messy hair sits atop his head, and those deep golden eyes pin me to the spot.

"I didn't think you'd try to get me drunk," I continue, dropping my gaze from his and making my way to the counter. Once I've found a small shot glass behind the bar, I fill it, and down another gulp of the strong alcohol. Patron is my choice of drink, especially when I need to forget.

He rises, still silent with the air of a predator, strolling over to me. Dressed in only his shirt and a pair of dark gray slacks, he looks ever the businessman, not the Dominant I know he is. Different to Nate, I know Carrick's needs, the control he holds onto so tightly is the only thing that I know he enjoys. He wields it like a blade, taking out his opponent—who is in this case, me—in one swoop. His sleeves are rolled up to his elbows, giving me a peek at the ink that adorns his left arm.

When he finally reaches me, he's still said nothing. Instead, he grabs my glass, fills it and downs the shot in one long gulp. I watch his throat work as he swallows, his Adam's Apple bobs up and down. He doesn't react, doesn't even wince at the harshness of the drink.

"I've always warned you never to love a man like me." Those are the first words he ever said to me when he'd finally lost all restraint with me one night. I was sixteen. He took my virginity when I sat on the hood of his car and opened my legs for him. I was in pain, I wanted him to take it away. The thing that most girl's hold as a prize, I gave away like it was a broken toy.

Where he found me, I wouldn't wish it on my worst enemy. My past was ugly, still is. My future isn't much brighter though. He'd walked into hell and stole me away. I had hearts in my eyes when he saved me. When he showed me that princes were real and they do slay the dragon, only Carrick didn't kill, he merely set two rules down on the table. If they were to come near me again, he'd have *his people* take care of them. And if any were to threaten me, even if it was from afar, he'd make sure they never saw the light of day again.

Even though I don't know much about him, about his past, I realized that night, there was something innately dangerous about the man who saved my life.

"Why, Eva?" he asks. He's genuinely curious, tipping his head to the side, watching me. I wish I could tell him what he wants to know, but I can't. I don't even know why I love Nate. Loved. Past tense.

"I want to forget, Carrick. Please, don't ask me to remember him. What we had." He sighs at me, he's disappointed. So am I. "There's only so much I can take right now and having you angry with me isn't one of those things," I tell him honestly. My rock. My sounding board through the life in this place, in this lifestyle and world where I find that emotions can not only hurt you, but turn you into someone you don't recognize.

"Why did you come up here, Eva? You know what I want."

"You asked me to meet you in your office," I sass him with my response. I'm hoping to taunt him, to make him want to spank me, but I know it will take a lot more than that. When I finally look into his honey-colored eyes, they're swirling with desire. "I want to play." The words fall from my lips with raw, pained honesty.

"I'm not taking you the day after the man you love walked out on you," he bites out. He's not angry at me, he's angry at himself. I watch him run his hand over the stubble on his jaw. He's the opposite of Nathan. In the dark, they both love the same world, but in the light of day, they couldn't be more different if they tried. And I wonder how they even know each other.

"Why? Are you scared? You're the only one who knows what I need right now." I tell him. I am single. He doesn't have to worry about Nate anymore. There's always been this underlying tension between us. I've never been in a real scene with him. Maybe tonight he'll help me forget.

"Eva, you don't know what you're asking," he warns. As always, he wants what's best for me. I don't. I need the pain to stop.

"I do. Carrick," I breathe. It's not seductive, it's pained. "Please just make the pain go away." This time, the pleading in my tone makes him narrow his eyes as he regards me warily for a long while. Perhaps he's waiting for me to change my mind. But I won't. We're in a standoff. I want him, he wants me, but there's an elephant in the room and it's my love for Nate. He knows it, and so do I.

"Strip. Down to your heels. Nothing else," he commands with the harshness I've been craving. Turning, he heads to the wall of toys that taunt me from their position.

Immediately, I slip the black dress I'm wearing down, it pools at my feet in a puddle of soft silk. Next, I step out of my panties and unclasp my bra. Once I'm naked, I pour another shot of tequila and down it immediately.

When I turn around, I'm met with the molten gaze of my knight in his Armani slacks, and a shirt that probably cost more than my damn apartment. Brutal, beautiful, and utterly enamored with me. The air is thick with lust. There's no love here, there's only the dark, sinful temptation of a man I shouldn't be with.

"Sit on my desk, lean back. Get those pretty red heels on the desk and spread your legs." The order is laden with his hunger. I stalk over to the mahogany desk that's empty except for his laptop that sits on the far end which is now closed. No more work tonight. For the rest of the evening, he'll have to be there for me. Allow me to cry, offer me physical release with the leather crop in his hands.

The desk is large with enough space for him to play. I settle back, leaning on my elbows. I lift my feet and set my heels on the edge. My legs spread lewdly for him. His honey-colored orbs turn to chestnut, and darker still as they roam over my curves, my smooth skin, and find my glistening core. In his hand, he grips the crop so tightly his knuckles turn white. I don't miss the small, infinitesimal smile that lifts his full lips. They're pink, soft, and in the shape of a Cupid's bow.

"It's been a long time since I've seen such a perfect woman. Elegant, sexy, and downright sinful," he murmurs reverently. That's when he offers me a full-on panty-melting smirk. One that would have most women kneeling for anything he's wanting to give. A curve on his lips is more intoxicating than the Patron I'd swallowed. "Are you sure you want this, Eva?"

I nod. I can't find the words. As much as I know that's what he needs from me, to hear my agreement, I can't give it to him.

He raises the small leather crop and brings it down hard on my mound. The sting sends me into orbit. My head drops back and I cry out his name. There's one thing I know about Carrick better than any other sub in this place, and that is he loves to hear his name being cried out in pain, or pleasure.

"Such a pretty cunt. I want to hurt it. You like when I hurt you. Don't you, Eva?" he questions once more, his voice thick and raspy. His gaze is locked on me, almost as if he needs to look at me to continue, to hold onto all his restraint.

"Yes, Carrick." I don't call him Sir because he doesn't own me. This isn't a Dom and sub, Master and slave, this is me and the man who stole my virginity when I offered it to him on a silver Mercedes Benz.

He brings the leather down, again and again, marking my body with it. The red welts rise on my smooth, tender skin. My clit throbs with need for this man. For him to take the ache in my chest and fuck it away.

"Carrick, please?" I plead like a wanton slut. He

halts all movements. His gaze penetrates me deeper than his cock ever could. Not because he's not well-endowed in the area, quite the opposite, but because he looks into my soul. He sees my pain. Like it's a living breathing entity between us. He understands, but there's one thing I know for certain about Carrick Anderson, and that is he will not fuck me. He knows my heart is filled with love for someone else. He'll whip me, spank me, hurt me, but he'll never give me anything more than that.

"Let's get a few things clear, Eva. Yes, I want to fuck you, perhaps more than any other woman in this fucking place." He gestures to the window, to the club below us. "But if I ever get the chance again, to shove my dick into your tight little cunt, it will be because you want me, not because I'm your source of relief from the ache of your heartbreak." Even though I expected it, his words are a blow to me. They slam into my chest, intensifying the ache that's so fresh.

I drop my legs, shutting myself off from him. He sees it immediately.

"Bend over my desk," he grunts, but I ignore the order, grabbing the dress I left on the floor. "Now." One word rumbled in *that* tone is all I need. I stalk over to his desk and bend at the waist, my naked breasts squashed on the wooden top. My hands grip the edges, knowing that something is coming. His foot kicks both mine apart, and once again, I'm open to him. "If you move, I'll make it hurt even worse than when I took your virginity," he promises.

I hear clicking, shuffling. I can't see what he's doing but the anticipation is too much. Then I hear the whoosh of thick leather. His belt. The burn catapults me into a dark abyss. The sting on my ass feels like he's just set my flesh alight. As if there's flames licking their way over the globes of my ass, he whips me, over and over again.

I raise up onto my toes with each lash. Tears stream from my eyes, but in the pain, I find solace for a moment. The agony that was gripping my chest in its vile claws release me into the space I need to feel at ease. To let go of Nate and to just be me.

When I hear the loud clank of the buckle falling to the floor, I sigh. Even though I want to, I don't move. Then his hands are on me. Massaging the cooling balm into the welts. His touch is gentle, a vast contrast to the way he just violently whipped me.

"You took twelve. It's a lot." His remark makes me smile through the discomfort. There's pride in his tone and I feel like I've done something right, for the first time in months. The burning sensation on my ass eases slightly from his attention, then he helps me up, offers me my dress which I slink into.

He hands me a shot glass filled to the brim which I accept gratefully.

"You need to rest. Go to my apartment, take two aspirin, and sleep. I'll be up in three hours." The keys he holds out to me are to the top floor of the building. Mason and Carrick both own penthouses above the club, but Carrick is the only one who stays here. I don't thank him. I don't respond because I don't need to. I take the keys and make my way to the door. Before I step out, he murmurs under his breath. "Fucking asshole." And I know he's feeling guilty for what he's just done.

SEVENTEEN

NATE

I haven't been to the club in two days. I couldn't bring myself to walk into the place knowing that she's there. Knowing she'll be on stage, introducing the live acts. Hearing her voice would set me off. I don't want another sub, slave, toy. I don't want any other woman, but Eva. And I can't have her.

If she finds out about what I did, why I was with her in the first place, she'll never forgive me. So, I've played out what I needed to for her to move on. What I did was wrong. How I treated her, when I realized I loved her, I knew I was fucked.

All my life I searched for the perfect woman. Not perfect physically, but emotionally. She was the one who gave me everything I needed. She was it for me. She obeyed, challenged, and made me want more. Most of all she accepted me for who I was. She saw the darkness in me and she gave it light, allowing me to finally feel at ease with who I am. I'd changed in the short time more so than I ever thought I would.

After the first week, I noticed it. I'd become more about her and less about sharing and humiliation. I didn't want to look at another woman. When we walked into Sins, it was Eva and me. Only us. That's all that mattered to me. Until my past reared its ugly head with a threat that would shatter her worse than I ever could. The agreement I'd signed came back to bite me in the ass. I sold my soul to the devil and I have no way of getting out of it.

Addiction, greed, and stupid choices brought me here. I've done this to myself. Making sure my future was secure in a career I'd always dreamed of, I realize now that money isn't all that matters. Allowing myself to feel, to show emotion was something I believed showed weakness. In my mind, love was unheard of. My desires and needs, made me different from an early age. When I first dominated a woman at the tender age of nineteen, I knew my life would never be the same. Degrading a woman, making her feel like less than nothing, was something I'd hungered for. Over time, I got worse, I fucked, I gambled, and I severed any emotional ties in my life.

Eva took what I gave her. She absorbed me like I was part of her and I believe without a doubt that she is, and will always be the other half of me, the missing piece that somehow fit in my fucked-up life. I sit back in my chair, and remember the second time I used her with another woman.

"This is going to be fun, Eva. Try for me?" She nods. *As we step into the room, I find another beautiful brunette kneeling for me. "I want you naked beside her," I tell my sweet slut. "Open your legs, Jessie," I order, the woman on her knees obeys, flashing me her clean shaven pussy. Smooth and tight. "Touch yourself. I want to see your juices drip onto the floor."*

I glance up for a moment, seeing the flashing lights. I know there's an audience. Eva settles beside our toy for the night, her gaze trained on me, awaiting instruction. I can see the trepidation in her gaze. She wants to please me, but doesn't want to share me. It doesn't work like that, sweetheart.

"Rub your pussy for me, sweet slut," I command Eva. She

moves her hand between her legs, tentatively stroking herself with her eyes never leaving mine. "Jessie, lie back, open your legs and get those ankles close to your ears. Eva is going to eat your cunt." That's when she shoots me daggers. Her blue eyes blaze with anger. "Are you embarrassed, slut?"

"No, Sir," she all but spits the words. Anger. So pretty on her. She moves to the woman who's lying on the plush carpet. I palm my dick, watching my beautiful woman lick the cunt of another. Her tongue laps at the wetness now glistening on Jessie's lips.

The sight is beautiful. I shove off my slacks, pushing my boxers down along with them. Once I'm naked from the waist down, my shirt still on, hanging open, I reach for Eva, tugging her up.

"On the bed." I pull Jessie up, moving her onto the black sheet that covers the mattress with her head hanging over the edge. Her mouth open and waiting for me. "Eat her cunt, sweetheart," I coo at Eva, watching shame paint her beautiful face. My cock throbs at her discomfort. I'm a vile person needing her like this. Aching for her to hate me, to get hard. There's no emotion. No affection. I hate myself enough as it is.

As soon as her mouth goes to work, I slam my hard cock

into Jessie's throat. The harsh sound of her gagging on my length only makes me want to ram in deeper. To see the spit dripping down her pretty face. My hips slam into her, using her mouth the same way I'd use her cunt. I reach for her nipples, twisting and tugging them harshly, almost violently as I gag her on the tip of my cock. Her screams are muffled by me and the vibration sends jolts of pleasure up my shaft.

"Do you want me to feed her my cum, sweetheart?" Eyes the color of the ocean drench me in their dangerous pull, the ebb and flow dragging me into their depths, drowning me. She glares at me angrily. Good girl, I want to murmur, but I don't. Pulling my cock from the woman's mouth, I fist it, watching Eva as she devours her first cunt. Licking and lapping at it like a kitten at a bowl of milk. "On the floor." In seconds, she's off the bed and at my feet, hungry for me. As I am for her.

As soon as her tongue darts out, her eyes trained on me, I shoot ropes of white seed on her face.

Painting her, marking her, and claiming her.

Mine.

The office is silent as I shake my head of the memory. That was one of many nights I spent with her, after we got home that night I fucked her until she couldn't move. She was limp in my arms, but she curled into me like I already owned her.

I thought I'd been clever, finished the agreement and moved on. When I got the call, I knew would come my resolve broke. I asked for time. But the benefactor wasn't going to let it go. She wouldn't allow it and I had to make a choice. Even though I denied it would happen, my past indiscretions finally caught up to me.

It's true what they say, all lies eventually come to light. Anything you hide behind will be seen. I knew soon Eva would learn that I knew who she was as soon as she told me her last name. By the time Marissa called me to give me a choice, it was too late to come clean. Too late to tell Eva everything. The only option I had was to walk away and keep her, and me safe.

Two long fucking days without her and I'm numb. The realization that I do love her, more than I ever let on, pulls me into the dark, and I don't know how I'm going to expel her from my heart and mind, or from the depth of my soul. She's more ingrained in me than I want to admit to myself, or to her. I haven't had a woman since

I walked out of the room leaving her with my release dripping from her pussy. I'm an asshole.

My phone buzzes on the desk, vibrating along the wooden surface. When I pick it up, I swipe across the screen to answer. "Carrick?"

"You've seriously fucked this up man," his thick English accent comes through the line in a heavy warning that's pure anger. I promised him I'd look after her, but all I've done was hurt her. He has every right to walk into this office and put a bullet in my head. I wouldn't fight him if he tried.

"Tell me something I don't know. I didn't have a choice. There wasn't a future for us," I respond, knowing he's not happy with the way I handled things.

"She is in my apartment. Came to me the day after you left wanting to play a scene. Begged me to in fact. She asked me to take her pain away," he informs me. His words set my blood to boil as jealousy lashes me with its venomous tongue.

"Excuse me?" I grit out through clenched teeth. I have no reason to be upset, I let her go. But the thought of his cock anywhere near her only serves to anger me.

"I didn't fuck her. However, I did whip her ass that night. I just wanted to let you know she's been staying with me since then. I can't let her go home alone." He sighs. "She's broken up over this, Nate. You need to sort your shit out." His warning is clear, I need to somehow find a way to make sure she's okay.

"There's no way I can be with her. I'm not—" My words are halted when I hear a soft voice on the other end of the line. It's her. Beside him. My grip on my phone is so tight I'm half expecting it to shatter or disintegrate.

"No, Eva. I'll be there now. Just go to bed," he tells her, the words are muffled and it sounds as if he's got his hand over the speaker. *Not well enough, Fucker!* "Sorry, I just think you need to sort this out. Talk. Just hear her out. Tell her what's going on, she'll understand."

"I can't. There's no way she'll understand what I did. What I had to do. If she finds out it will hurt her even more and I can't see that happen."

He chuckles wryly down the line. "So, it's okay for everyone else to see her hurt? You're a fucking pussy man. This woman loves you. And if you don't make her yours, claim her, I promise you, someone else will very fucking soon." He doesn't need to tell me that he's talking about himself. Because I know he wants her.

"Fuck you, Carrick. If you put your dick anywhere near her, I'll slice it off with no qualms." My words are poison, spat out in anger. When Eva told me she and Carrick were an item, it took all my restraint not to find him and kill him. I'm not good with jealousy. I'm the asshole that thinks if he can't have you no one else will. Even though I walked out on her knowing she'd go to him, the reality is far more painful than I thought it would be.

"If she's begging for it, I'm not going to deny a beautiful woman," he says confidently, before hanging up, leaving me raging. Just then, my office door opens and in strolls the source of all this shit.

"Nathan, nice to see you again." She's dressed in a red two-piece business suit, skirt and jacket with a white blouse beneath. Her lips are fire-engine red, and her shoes match the outfit. Her long dark hair is pinned in a tight bun, making her face look severe. Botox, plastic surgery, everything about her is fake and in my desperation, I didn't see it. Her eyes are a dark blue, but they shoot fire when she lays them on me. A viper. A poisonous snake. When I agreed to her contract, I sold my soul to the devil, and right now, she's standing in my office.

"What do you want? I've done what you asked me. It's over between Eva and I," I inform her in frustration. She slinks into the chair opposite my desk and watches me with a satisfied smirk. A woman of power. The only person who can force me to walk away from the woman I love.

"I've come to see how you're handling not being around the little slut." The snake before me spits her venom. Rising from my seat, I round my desk. Leaning in, I grip her neck, lifting her from the seat. I watch as the pupils of her blue eyes dilate with excitement.

"If you ever call her that again, I'll make sure that you're six-feet under with no one standing beside your filthy grave. You got what you wanted. Two long fucking years of my life you've been in charge, you've ruled over me with that fucking list of yours because I was stupid enough to listen to you. No more. You will leave Eva alone, she has nothing to do with our agreement." When I release her, I step back, watching her smirk as if she's won the goddamn jackpot.

"Nathan Ashcroft, there's nothing you can threaten me with. I have proof of you taking the money. So, if you'd like your sweet Eva to find out what a piece of filth you are I can make that happen with one message. And I can't imagine she'd want anything to do with you if she knew. Do you?" She steps by me, heading to the window. Her gaze trained on the city below. "She's a sweet girl, you know." Her words soften as she turns to me again. "She doesn't deserve someone like you, but if you feel differently by all means. Go ahead, tell her what a greedy piece of shit you are. And because you like to play in those voyeur rooms, I have some beautiful footage of the type of monster you are," she informs me, causing my blood to run cold. Of course, she's got evidence of that, because she's the one who loves to be the voyeur. If there was a way to get her in that room, I'd have leverage, but I know she's too cunning to fall for a plot like that.

Her expression turns evil, sinister in the worst way and I know she's not joking. I'm not good for Eva. I've gambled my way to the bottom, and when Marissa walked into my life offering me a way out, I took it. She gave me the money to keep A&B Finance afloat, but in return she gave me a list of girl's names, only their first name and a photo. Women she told me needed to be taught a lesson. You see, Marissa is a special sort of vile creature. She gets off watching the humiliation of slaves, submissives.

If Eva ever found out why I went into Sins that night to ask for her specifically because I'd had a list that had her name on it, she'd never talk to me again. She was my last slave to degrade. She was the one who sealed the contract that I wouldn't lose my business. I knew her before I'd even laid eyes on her. But the problem is, Eva finding out would cause her to hate me for other reasons entirely.

I never told Asher, or anyone for that matter, what I did. Losing five-million dollars of one of our top clients would have put me under. My gambling debt was out of control. And in walked Marissa Gallagher. She knew I was a Dominant, because she'd watched me. Calculating. Cold. A hunter. And for once in my life, I was the prey.

My greed for money put me in her line of sight.

My need for humiliation and degradation made me perfect for her plan.

And it was my downfall.

And I broke the only jewel I ever owned.

EIGHTEEN

EVA

The dungeon is quiet, but I feel him behind me. I always sense him walk into a room. We've been tethered to each other since we first laid eyes on the other. Since the first time I kneeled for him, I knew there was something different about Nathan Ashcroft and I knew the moment he spanked me, I was hooked. His power, that commanding force that follows him like a fog leaves me desperate for more.

A week has passed with soft kisses, harsh spanks, and Nathan taking me every which way he can. Last night he was sweet and loving, and no doubt tonight he'll need the rough and hard. I've become accustom to his mood swings. The emotion that somehow thunders in his words, yet swirls in his eyes. He needs this, I need this, but I know as each day passes, every time he takes me, I want more. And with each spank, each moment that we connect, he craves it too.

He's my high and I'm addicted. I'm currently kneeling

in the dungeon, naked, with my legs spread, my hands on my thighs palms facing up. It's not cold, but my nipples are hard from a slight chill. My long dark hair is bound in blood red silk rope. There are intricate patterns that bind around my chest, just beneath my breasts forming a star. My calves are bound to my thighs as I kneel, so I can't move unless he unties me. He's been working on Shibari, learning from Mason and testing it out on me. The feel of the soft rope on my fevered skin is phenomenal.

"Is my sweet slut wet?" he asks from behind me. The name he's gifted me happened the first night we were together. At first, I thought he called all his sub's that, but I realized soon enough, I'm special. He only calls me that.

"Yes, Sir," I respond easily, a small smile playing on my lips. My voice already raspy with need. He walks around me, inspecting me in my presentation pose. When he crouches, his index finger tilts my chin up. Those dark eyes meet mine. He reaches for the rope that holds my legs in place and unbinds them swiftly with a tug. Once I'm free, I drop my eyes again.

"You look beautiful, stand," he orders firmly. But the praise doesn't go unnoticed.

"Thank you, Sir," I whisper, standing to full height, but

I don't meet his gaze again. He didn't ask me to and I know I have to obey. This life wasn't my first choice, I kind of fell into it. I never thought of myself as submissive until I met Carrick. I was sixteen. He taught me light BDSM by cuffing me to his bed, he spanked me, edged me, and I was hooked.

Nate stalks behind me, gripping my long plait, he tugs it back so my neck is stretched to his mercy. "I feel like devouring you tonight. Walk to the window, place both your hands on the glass, do not hide your body. If our neighbors see you, too fucking bad." His voice is warm, like a blanket covering me in its safety. His tone is rich, like the smooth brandy he loves to drink. And his lips on the shell of my ear as he gives his order is like a match is being struck and I'm the wick.

There's a storm raging around us, but inside me, it coils in my stomach, tightening deliciously with the anticipation of what's to come. What incredible pleasure I know he'll bestow on my trembling body.

The thing about Sir is that he likes humiliating me. Degradation. One of the kinks that so few I've met enjoy. When I lean forward, I take in the city below me—cars passing, people walking hand in hand and here I am about to be tortured.

"Are you ready to go into subspace my slut?"

"Yes, Sir." The thought of him taking me there again has my body pulsing with need. I've only ever been in that state once before. I hear him shuffle behind me, the toys he's going to use are set out beside me on the table and I know I'm in for it.

"Hold on to that window, if you slip, you'll get ten more," he warns and I know he's not joking. Lightly, he strokes the paddle over my bare ass, the wood is cool to my heated skin sending goosebumps racing over my flesh as it tingles in anticipation. As soon as the paddle is lifted from my ass, I shut my eyes and wait for the sting.

Left. Right. Left. Right.

Again and again.

I lose count. I lose all ability to think, to talk, to move.

My skin is on fire, smarting, but I don't move. He doesn't stop, I don't ask him to relent. I don't even call "yellow" to tell him I'm close to my limit. Only because I need to go there. To the place where I'm safe, where all my fears, all the pain goes away.

"My sweet little slut," he coos the filthy name. "You love my mark. Don't you?" I can't respond, he knows I can't. My mind is already flying. Then I feel him move, the buzz of a vibrator sounds around us, but I'm long gone. Floating, flying.

The plastic touches my sodden pussy, finding my throbbing clit and I cry out his name to the city who watch from below me. "Good girl, but you better not come or I'll stop all this," he murmurs his threat in that thick seductive tone. He continues his assault on my ass, and his taunting on my wet slit, but I know I have to refrain from allowing the pleasure to take over completely. I know I can't fall over the edge or I'll be in a world of pain.

"Sir, please," I bite out, not angrily, merely in frustration. My nails dig into the window, but he doesn't tell me to come. He holds me on edge. Lifting the vibrator, he halts his spanks and my body trembles. I need more, less, something in between. I don't know. As I slowly come down from the high, he starts the torture again sending me skyrocketing toward the edge, I'm standing there, waiting to fall, to fly, to move. But as I hold onto that feeling, he stops again.

I think I growl, I can't be sure, but a sound vibrates deep in my throat. He doesn't let off, he keeps me hovering on the precipice. The vibrator on my clit, the spanks with the paddle, it's the only contact he's making with my body. My core is dripping, I can feel my arousal on my inner thighs. Sticky, warm, I'm about to lose it. I know I am.

"Do you want to come, slut?" he asks, I think he's laughing, but I'm too delirious to tell.

"Yes, Sir!" I cry out.

"No. You're a horny little fuck toy that I need to use some more." His words only send me spiraling into the abyss of dark desire, and dangerous lust.

Once again, he starts his assault. My ass smarts. My clit feels as if it's about to explode. My body is wound so tight, everything south of my belly button feels as if it's being gripped in a tight fist.

My knees wobble, my thighs tremble. I bite down on my lip, I can't hold on anymore and he knows it. As soon as I feel myself slipping, the command comes. "Squirt for Sir. Soak the floor in your sweet cunt juices." He growls and I do. My body releases from the coil and I snap. My cries are so harsh, so loud I'm sure the people from seven floors down can hear me.

I shut my eyes so tight, all I see is white, harsh and bright, but it only makes me squeeze them tighter. My knees shake, my hands slide down the window as I collapse onto all fours, slipping on the wooden floor where I've drenched it in my slick release.

"Now lick up the mess you made, then come and kiss

me." He settles beside me on the floor waiting as I lick up what I can. My body trembling from the orgasm. As soon as he's happy with what I'm doing, he pulls me into his arms, cocooning me from the hurt and pain of life, giving me the affection I crave in that moment. My mind isn't here. It's floating far above us. The moment is perfect. His arms are warm, he offers affection, safety and I know as I come down from that place, he'll be there to hold me. Giving me the aftercare of a caring, affectionate Dominant.

When I wake from the dream, the memory of that night when I had his arms around me, I find the bedroom draped in darkness. Carrick must be at work. My ass is still sore from when he whipped me. In a way, I'm glad he didn't take me. Yes, I wanted it. Wanted him, but in my heart, I know I'll never belong to any other man, but Nathan.

I swing my legs over the edge of the bed, pushing up onto wobbly limbs. I've slept more in the last two days than I have in months. Deciding I need something warm to drink, I head down the long hallway to the kitchen. The place is meticulous and I almost feel bad for dirtying a mug, but I set it on the counter, turn on the kettle, and watch the water boil through the glass jug.

My mind has been in turmoil and my body has been in pain. Nothing can prepare you for having someone you love walk out on you. But deep down, I have a feeling that Nate wasn't telling me everything. Perhaps he really doesn't love me, but why wait three long weeks to get rid of me. I don't understand why he didn't just break up with me, like a normal person would, tell me to move on. Why try to hurt me. It doesn't make sense that he wanted me to feel anger, or even hatred toward him.

There's one thing I know about him is that he doesn't do something without reason. That means there's more to this whole situation than he's told me. Determination is a dangerous thing when you're in pain. It makes you do things you probably shouldn't. My mind reels with confusion. I need to do something. Force him to tell me the truth. But how? The kettle clicks once it's boiled, and I fill the mug with steaming liquid.

"He still loves you," a voice from behind startles me and I spin around to find Carrick leaning against the door frame looking ever the sex god in his charcoal suit and silver dress shirt. His hair is messy, sticking up in all directions making it look like he's been pulling at it in frustration.

"What makes you think that?"

Sighing, he pushes away from the door, shoving his hands in the pockets of his slacks. "I called him. I needed to know what the fuck is going on. Something doesn't sit well with me and I wanted to know how he could let you go. Granted, I don't care, because I'd rather have you in my bed than his, but I can see you're broken up about this."

"You had no right—"

"I have every fucking right, Eva," his voice is steel. Hard and cold like the man himself. Carrick is a cold-hearted bastard and I don't understand how he can care for me when I've never seen him with a woman more than once. He fucks around like it's his job. He over-indulges with women in this club like they're all here for him. As if he wants to test every submissive in the country so he can boast about having her first.

With me he can.

"I didn't mean to get angry, I just don't like seeing you hurt," he confesses, his tone gentler now. I stalk toward him, gripping my mug. The heat of it warming me, but I'm still cold. It feels as if it's seeped into my bones somehow and I don't know how to change that. How do I find warmth again, when it walked out of my life?

"I'm not yours to care for, Carrick. You let me go years ago. We may still be friends, but you need to let me fight my own battles. If he wanted to leave, then I couldn't stop him."

"Six years I've watched you, Eva. I've seen you flourish from that broken teenager to a woman who can hold her own. Do you not think somewhere in that time I've come to care for you?" He grips my hips, holding me steady because I feel like I'm about to faint. His touch is something else entirely, not lustful, but kind, affectionate.

"You told me when I was seventeen that you couldn't be with me. Even though I wanted you. I was ready to submit to you," I tell him, meeting gentle eyes.

"You were a child," he hisses.

"I wasn't a child when you fucked me on the hood of your Mercedes Benz that night," I counter quickly.

I know I'm pushing him, but I have nothing left. Only him.

"Don't tempt me to put you over my knee and spank that sass out of you, girl. Because I will and I'll enjoy it." His feral growl is enough to send a shudder racing down my spine. Those deep honey-colored eyes bear down on me, staring into me, seeing my anguish. "This isn't you. It never was. Yes, you may enjoy kneeling, spanking, and submitting, but you're no slave."

"I was to him," I say, lifting my chin in defiance. I may not have been used to the kink that Nathan enjoyed, but I wanted to because of him. I wanted the man, the monster, all the sides of him he kept hidden beneath a suit and tie. He had a polished exterior, but was so broken inside. Just like me. We were two halves of the same broken glass. We fit together seamlessly. Only, the glue that once held us somehow disintegrated and we're once again left forgotten shattered pieces.

"To him you were a fucking toy!" He roars, pivoting so fast, I feel dizzy. His fist slams into the wooden door, breaking through the surface. When he pulls it back out, blood oozes from his knuckles. Grabbing the tea towel, I race to him, taking his hand in mine. When I dab at the blood he hisses. Gently, I pull a splinter from his finger causing him to growl like a rabid dog. "You see what you are?"

Snapping my gaze to his, I stare at him for a moment before asking. "What?"

"You my sweet girl," he whispers, cupping my face with his other hand like I'm fragile, "are a submissive. You want to please. That's why you did what you thought he needed. Did you enjoy when he fucked other women with you right there?" I shake my head, biting my bottom lip to keep it from trembling. "I'm a Dominant, I can give you what you need," he assures me. His gaze imploring, and as much as I want that, as much as I crave to be needed, wanted, desired, there's only one man that pulls at my heart.

"Carrick," I breathe softly in a gentle warning. I know we can't do this. I wanted it before, but now that it's right here in front of me, I know we don't belong together. My emotions are all over the place, playing with me in ways I can never fathom, but I can't fuck up my friendship with Rick. So, I offer a small smile. "I can't. I'll always belong to him." Moments pass. Then he nods.

"I'll go. Make yourself at home. I need space." Then he turns and leaves me standing in his kitchen with a bloody tea towel and my heart thudding against my ribs. Sighing, I drop the cloth on the countertop and head into his bedroom to find my belongings. Pulling my phone from my purse, I scroll down to Nate's number and hit dial. I'm not sure what I'm going to say to him, but it's time we sit down and talk like adults. On the fourth ring, I'm about to hang up when he finally answers.

"What?"

"Nathan?" His breathing hitches at the sound of my voice. He must've answered without looking at his phone, or he'd already deleted my number. The latter makes my heart ache.

"Eva, why are you calling me?" He sounds like he's walking. The noise from the traffic sounds over the line and I can't help wondering where he's going. Jealousy tingles through me, taunting me. Perhaps he's going to meet another woman. Someone who can give him what he needs.

Steeling my voice, I breathe deeply before responding. "We need to talk."

"There's nothing more to say. We don't work. This is finished, Eva. I made myself clear, or did you not feel degraded enough when I left you thoroughly fucked with cum dripping from your cunt?"

His words are meant to hurt and sting. Instead they enrage me. "No, clearly I didn't. I guess I'll take Carrick up on his offer then since you're—"

"What?" he demands. His voice is shrill, losing his confident cocky edge. I can hear the fear lacing his shocked grunt.

My mind works quickly. I'm about to goad the beast and I know it's wrong, but I'm angry. I need to finally fight for what I want. And I want Nathan. If that means taunting him the way he did to me, then so be it. I'm no longer the scared little girl that's happy to take his shit.

The man I want is a monster, but I've seen him in another light too. I've gotten glimpses of his romantic side, the tender, gentler side. That's the Nathan I want and that's what I'm about to go to war for.

"You heard me. Carrick offered me his Dominance.

He's told me that he's prepared to collar me." My confidence slips when a sound falls from his mouth that is inhumane. I know I'm about to put myself in a world of hurt, but I no longer care. Suddenly, a door shuts somewhere and I hear an engine rev in the background.

"If you go anywhere near him, mark my words, I'll cane you. Not only your ass, but your tits and cunt too. You'll be in so much pain, for so fucking long, you'll forget that any other man exists but me. Do you understand me, Eva? I'm not playing around. His cock, his hands, any of his fucking toys touch you in any way, I'll make sure you pay for it."

"Jealousy never did look good on you, Nathan. It doesn't feel good being played at your own game, does it?" I don't know where I find my self-confidence, but it seems to spark me into action. I'm pulling on a pair of jeans and my trainers by the time Nate hangs up in a fit of rage with threats of killing Carrick. I race down the stairs only to slam into Mason's hard body. He's built like a goddamn wall. Tall, dark, and handsome, he's all sorts of exotic with his European ancestry.

"Woah, pretty lady." His hands grab me, holding

me from falling back onto my ass. "Are you okay?"

Nodding quickly, I ask. "Where's Rick?" My breath coming out in short spurts. Fear than Nathan will harm Carrick sets me into a panic that is too confusing to think about.

"He's in the office. Are you okay?"

I don't respond, but offer a small smile. As I push past him, I head straight for the dark wooden door at the end of the hallway. Shoving it open, I gasp when I find Carrick balls deep inside Jessie. The same girl that Nate made me go down on.

"Shit," Rick hisses, pulling out of the bent over brunette. "Leave." He growls at her, and I notice the glare she pins me with. She quickly pushes the hem of her dress down which was bunched around her waist and scurries by me with a huff. Once we're alone, and he's safely tucked in his slacks, he pins me with a questioning gaze. "You want a ride as well? Bent over or...?" He laughs, amusement written all over his face.

"I told Nate you offered to collar me," I inform him, ignoring the question. He reaches up, running his fingers through his already sex-mussed hair.

"Jesus, Eva." He flops into the chair as I close the door with a resounding click.

"He's on his way here to kill you." My teeth pull on my lower lip, biting down hard in fear at the thought of what Nathan is capable of. Carrick watches me for a moment before rising confidently. He heads toward me, gripping my shoulders, he holds me to him, pulling me into a warm embrace. He's so calm and my anxiety is spiked. My stomach is in knots with thoughts of what is about to happen. I wanted a reaction from Nathan, I'm sure to get one now.

"I'll move mountains for you, Eva. And trust me when I say, I'm not scared of him," he assures me as the door flies open and we both turn to find the livid, rage-filled mocha eyes of Nathan Ashcroft.

NINETEEN

"Get the fuck off her," I roar. My vision blurs in anger at seeing another man's hands on what's mine. Even though I walked away, Eva will always belong to me. Stepping into the office, I slam the door shut, pinning my glower on Carrick. He doesn't look worried that I'm about to rip him a new asshole.

"Nate, please?" When Eva's voice cuts through my anger, I snap my gaze to her. She's staring at me like I'm the bad guy. Perhaps I am, but she pushed me to do this. To be here fighting for her.

"What? You want to fuck him?" I gesture to Carrick who's standing there with a knowing smirk on his face. He did this on purpose. Overconfident fucking asshole.

"Carrick, please give us a moment?" She turns to him, looks at him like he's her knight in Armani armor. He nods once, leaning in, he plants a kiss to her forehead, keeping his eyes trained on me. Taunting me. When he strides by me, his eyes never leave mine. He leaves us in his office without a word, but the warning was clear in the look he gave me. I know he doesn't trust me with her. I don't blame him. The door clicks closed behind me, but I don't move. This is her doing, so she's in control, for once.

When I finally turn to face her again, I meet her stare. "What did you do that for? Did you want me to come here and hurt you again?"

"No, Nathan. I wanted to see if you even felt something for me. And you being here, shows how much you care for me, and don't fucking look at me like that." She waves her hand in the air. "As much as you deny it, your racing here to rip me from Carrick's arms shows how much you actually want me. So, why don't you quit playing games and tell me what the fuck is going on?"

Her body visibly shakes. As the tremors shoot through her all I want to do is go to her and pull her into my arms where she belongs, but I can't. I need us to sort through this shit to get to that point. "I can't take the thought of another man touching you, Eva," I confess honestly. It's the most I can give her, I wish she'll let it go. But I know her too well.

"That doesn't make sense. You don't want me, so nobody can have me?" I'm being unfair. I know this. Who knew it was so difficult to let go. "You're happy to share yourself with other women while I watch, but if I went to another Dominant, it didn't matter who, you'd be jealous. And we're not even together. How is that fair?" She stalks toward me then, raising her hand, she swings, slapping me hard across the face. "Do you know what it did to me watching you fuck other women? Using them. Letting them suck your cock? Let me tell you one thing, Nathan, you're a fucking coward. You can't even get hard without hurting me. Without breaking me down. That doesn't make you a Dominant. Or a Master. That makes you a fucking pussy ass coward. That's what you are," she spits the words at me, fire blazing through them, flames licking at me as she tears me down, and I deserve every fucking moment. "And until you decide to change, to give me the honesty you owe me, we are done. And I will go to Carrick and ask him to take me on as his submissive."

Her words fuel the anger inside me, but I don't lash out, I don't respond because everything she says is true. I see our relationship through her eyes and I wonder how she doesn't hate me. How she's standing here talking to me.

"I'm a selfish bastard."

"Yes, that you are," she tells me confidently, in her raging, yet honeyed tone. Even when she's livid she's beautiful, a fucking diamond in my darkness. My jewel.

"I've had a problem for a long time. My greed, my addiction, it made me blind to everything around me. Including you. When I walked into Seven Sins, I saw you and I had to have you," I tell her with more honesty than I've ever allowed myself to give anyone. I should tell her. She needs to know what I've done. Why I found her, but I can't because she's right, I am a coward.

"Look, I can't be yours if you're going to go out fucking other women. I can't share you. I gave you me, all of me and you took it and flushed it down the drain. I watched with each scene how you enjoyed those women. Sadly, I can't give you what you need. And I know that's why you left. I—"

"NO!" I halt her words immediately. "That's not why I walked out. I…" This is it. Do or die. If I tell her the truth, she'll hate me, but at least she'll know I did love her enough to leave. "I left because I'm not good enough for you. Because I lied to you when we first met."

"What?" she asks, shock dripping from the word, burning through my heart. Her eyes are wide, big blue orbs filled with pain. "You mean the night you asked Carrick to send me to room one?" Her question is filled with confusion. I nod, looking out through the glass at the club below, I can't help watching the people move around, sip their drinks, enjoy their time with partners, subs and Doms.

This life, it's not for the feint hearted. It's a cold, cruel world and I've turned into that. I've become closed off. But when Eva strolled into my life, she did something no other woman could. She broke through those high walls I'd built, she'd seen the ugliness inside me and she loved me anyway.

"Two years ago, I was in financial debt. I was about to lose the company, but it wasn't just mine because my best friend trusted me enough to partner with me and if

I went down, Asher would too. I didn't have a choice, I was pushed into a corner and I made the wrong choice. My greed sent me spiraling down a dark hole and when I saw light, it was in the form of a check. Attached to that piece of paper was an agreement." I allow my words to stop for a moment, for her to hear what I'm saying. To try to piece together my past.

Deep down, I want her to fall into my arms once I've confessed and tell me it's going to be okay. For the first time in all my life, I want to collar a submissive. I want to claim her and no other. My chest aches, tightens painfully as I recall how much Evangeline Gallagher means to me. And how much she's about to hate me.

"I took the money, I agreed to come in here and find you. I agreed to hurt you in the voyeur room. I said yes to degrading you, humiliating you. In the same room where people can watch and get off on the shit going on inside. She knew I was a monster and she took that as her in to drag me into this sick plan of hers."

"I don't understand. Who are you talking about?"

I can't look at her, so I drop my gaze to the floor. I watch her shoes move into my line of sight. She's imploring me to meet her eyes, but I can't. I can feel her heated stare on me. It's burning a hole right through me.

"She wanted to see you suffer. I don't know why, I didn't ask." I shake my head in frustration at my stupidity. "But after that first night, I couldn't stay away from you, so I told her that I was done with you, that one night was a once off."

I finally lift my head to face Eva. I want to reach for her, but it's too dangerous. We'll both hurt each other and that's not what I want.

"She believed me until she walked in here last week. We were leaving after playing a scene. I received a call that evening at my office, telling me that if I don't let you go, she'll expose who I really am. She's threatening to take my company, to tell you I'd taken money to fuck you, and I have no way to change her mind. I didn't realize who she was to you until you told me your name."

"Nate, nothing you're saying is making sense. Who is this woman? She's blackmailing you. It's illegal. Why me? I'm so confused nothing you're saying is actually an explanation to why you left. What she's doing is wrong, you can report her. You can go to the—"

"I can't go to anyone. If I do, she will sell the photos and videos she has of me in the dungeon to the papers. I'll lose everything."

Eva steps forward then, she doesn't reach for me, she only looks into my eyes. "It sounds to me like you've already lost everything that means something to you." Her honesty is jarring.

"Yes, I have. I want you, Eva. You're my everything. Since the moment I laid eyes on you, the only person who's ever accepted me for who I am and not for what I can give them. The only woman I want in my arms, in my home, and in my bed. I need you, my beautiful diamond." I implore her with a gaze. I pin her in place with a look that tells her I love her. I've never said the words to anyone. But I want to say them to her. Not now. This isn't the right time. I want her to be with me because she wants to be, not because I'm telling her what she wants to hear.

"Then tell me who this woman is that's doing this to you? Nate, if you want this to work, if you really want a second chance, then you need to trust me."

She's right. I do. I need to let go of the fear of people

walking out on me. To steel myself from having that happen, over the years I've made sure that I was the one to walk out. Now, I have a choice.

"Marissa Gallagher," the words fall from my mouth, effortlessly yet painfully. Slowly, her gaze glosses over, tears fill those beautiful blue orbs and they shimmer as she regards me.

"My… my fucking mother? Did you…? Oh, God…" she murmurs while stepping back, not finding the words I know she's dying to ask. I should answer. Put her out of her misery, but I don't. I'm an asshole like that, so I watch her stumble over the question. "You… Did you? You and her?" Her face is filled with torment so pained, that I feel it in my chest.

With Eva, every emotional scar I'm causing her, is one I'm carving into my own soul.

"Answer me!" Her screech is loud, it bounces off the walls causing me to step closer to her which is a mistake. Her hand comes out again, but this time I'm too fast. Before she can make contact with my face, I grip her wrist, pulling her against me. The tears she held back all this time fall, they race down her pink cheeks in trails of salty emotion.

"I have never been with her, never laid a hand on her. She and I never fucked. There's this strange addiction that she has to seeing women, submissives she chooses debased. Degraded," I utter, as bile rises in my throat, causing me to want to kill for the woman in my arms. She shuts her eyes to my gaze and I miss the blue, the pools of torment that I caused. "Eva, please look at me."

"I can't, Nate. I can't do this. That money that paid off your debt, that was money you took to fuck me. To hurt me. To humiliate me in front of her, all for what? Did she tell you why she was doing it? Did she explain why she is so angry at me?"

I shake my head, but I know she can't see it, so I give her the honest answer. "No, I didn't know who you were to her until you told me your last name. I had no idea why, or how, all I knew was I had to do what she asked."

She's silent for a moment, and I feel the tension radiating from her. "So you knew most of the time we were together who I was, but you didn't once think to say anything?"

"Eva, I was scared of losing you. I realize now how

stupid that might sound, but seeing you walk out the door was something I couldn't bring myself to see." My voice is raspy as the guilt chokes me with a vice like grip.

"When my father died he left all his assets to me. Money beyond my wildest imagination. A week after his funeral just after they read the Last Will and Testament, that's when she reappeared in my life. It was sudden that she was back in the picture. After all those years, leaving me with him, walking out on her family. Apparently, somehow, she had heard through the grapevine that I was about to inherit a fortune, she decided to play the doting mother."

Eva doesn't look at me as she tells me her story. Her truth. And I have a feeling this is going to gut me more than anything I've ever been through.

"She had lawyers who fought that she was my legal guardian which allowed her to take hold of all that money I had from my dad. Slowly, she swindled it into foreign accounts I can't find. I never told anyone about this, Carrick knows what she made me do, what she and her vile filth of a partner made me do. I had to stop him from murdering them in cold blood that night. I was forced out of the home my dad gave me when Carrick found me."

"What did they do to you? Why are you so broken, my beautiful diamond?" I ask. When I reach for her, she doesn't move. "I want to know. I've trusted you, please trust me. This," I gesture between us as I cup her cheek in my hand, "is not ending. I can't live without you, Eva. I know I can't. But I want you to tell me what happened to you. We can work through this, if you can forgive me, if you can find it in your heart to see past my mistake, we'll figure this out."

She darts her gaze to me. For a moment, I think she's going to deny me, but she closes her mouth again, as if considering my words. It feels as if I'm standing on a goddamn cliff about to jump. If she refuses me, I'm not sure how I'd walk out of here. But I'll never give up fighting for her.

"Eva, you are my everything. Mine. No one else's. You know that and so do I. Even if you walk out here right now, I'll find you, I'll fight for you, and make no mistake, I'll hurt, maim, or kill anyone who stands in my way."

She inhales a deep breath, and then utters her confession with raw, agonizing honesty. "When my mother brought home her partner as she called him, Morgan was nice, he was friendly. But I didn't realize what they'd gotten themselves into. He slowly became more..." Her words trail off and I know immediately what she's not telling me. My blood pressure hits an all-time high as I see red. I see fucking death before me and it's going to be by my hand. "It was the night of my sixteenth birthday everything changed. They said they were throwing me a party. But it was the night my mother really started showing her true colors. They had invited so called friends that..."

She breaks then, Eva fucking shatters and falls into my arms like a rag doll. I'm holding her up, scooping her into my arms, I walk over to the sofa and sit down with her curled in my lap.

"Morgan had a few friends over, they were sniffing coke off the dining room table. The same table where my father and I used to have dinner."

"Eva—"

"Th-they paraded me in front of those men, six of

them sat and ogled me," her voice cracks and I feel the pain in my own throat. "Their hands... Morgan said he'd make sure when by the time I was eighteen that I knew what a whore felt like."

"What the fuck did your mother do?"

Her gaze lifts then, meeting mine with acute torment in those blue eyes. "Nothing. I was forced to watch her fuck those men while they groped and grabbed me. She enjoyed it. That's when I ran."

I'm close to exploding, to fucking breaking something, someone. And I know who's going to help me sort this bitch out. Marissa will fucking pay and when she does I'll be there to watch her fall so far down the abyss of degradation and torture. And I'll smile.

Her confession cracks through the concrete walls that I've built around my heart and I know it's time. Right here, right now. I need to do it.

"I love you, Eva. I want nothing more than to call you mine. I swear on all I'm worth, I'll make her pay for what she did to you. Her and that piece of filth. But I want us to do it together. Be mine. Please? Let me be your knight this time, not Carrick, not anyone else. I'll prove to you I'm worthy of you, your submission, and everything that comes along with it. But most of all, I want to hold that beautiful heart you keep locked away in my hands. To keep it safe from breaking. Will you give it to me?"

A moment of clarity attacks me with vengeance and I know what I need to do. I lift her, setting her on the sofa and for the first time in my life I drop to my knees. I kneel for a woman. I submit to her instead of the other way around.

Her gasp is soft, a gentle sound that seems to lull me into a cocoon of safety. Confidence soars as I reach into my pocket and hold up the long velvet box which holds the gift I bought before I walked out and left her. I was always too scared to give it to her. Too scared to admit I wanted her as mine.

"Nate," she says in a tone filled with surprise. Sadness no longer lingers in her blue eyes and I intend to keep it that way. Forever.

"Eva," I respond. We don't need words. Since the first night we met, we never needed to say anything. Our souls converse in ways that our mouths cannot.

My own fear of loving her is gone. Now, all bets are off. She takes the box, snapping it open. An inhale of surprise is the only thing I hear. A smile lingers on her full pink lips. The silver collar with a small heart locket that's been engraved for her sits nestled in the black velvet. *Nate's Sweet Slut.* It's the only name I've ever called her in our scenes because she is mine.

TWENTY

EVA

I want to turn away, I should turn away. Tell him no. After all the pain and agony, I should run a mile. But in doing that, I'll only allow the hold that bitch has over me to continue. My mother's done so much to me. Hurt me in ways I couldn't even begin to explain. Now's my chance to face my past, or keep running. It's time to either walk into the storm with my hand in Nate's and my feet firmly on the ground, or I can be the spineless bitch she called me all those years ago.

I don't blame Nathan. Deep in my heart I know what she's capable of. I've been her toy for far too long. It's time for me to fight back, to take my life into my hands.

A calmness settles over me. If I'm smart, I'll tell him to move on and I'll do the same. But, I've never been smart. I've always listened to my heart. And right now, as I meet his imploring gaze, having him kneel for me, I know I'm going to agree to go with him.

He took money to hurt me. To shatter me for a woman who hates me. I knew one day she'd find me. Her cold heartless demeanor had been her downfall. She never had love in her life. And she made sure no one else around her did either. When my father died I was alone, until the wicked witch walked back in and took everything from me.

I grew up not knowing what a mother's love or affection was. When I finally ran, I packed my backpack with some clothes stuffed into the space along with my toothbrush and my notebook. I left everything behind and let her have it. Money never meant anything to me, all I wanted was my dad. After what she did to me, what Morgan did to me, I knew I'd never know what family is.

The night of their so-called party, when those filthy men groped me. Their vile hands on parts of my body, fingers prodding me, grabbing my breasts, spitting disgusting words. It was then I knew if I didn't get out I'd lose more than just my virginity. I'd lose my soul in the process.

When I met Carrick, he promised to care for me. To make sure nothing harmed me in any way, and he kept that promise. He found me out of my mind from the tequila I inhaled like it was giving me my next breath and the coke I'd shoved up my nose. He dragged me to the parking lot of the club I'd almost been raped in and slapped some sense into me.

He was my new family. Sex wasn't anything special to me anymore. It was a means to an end. My end. The girl that my dad raised died, and in her place, was a cold woman who needed the pain to forget. My story isn't filled with sweet words and roses, it's the whips, chains, and degradation that make me forget. When I knew what I needed to do, it came easily to me.

That night I finally let go of my past, I begged Rick to take me. I slutted myself out to a man who acted like my knight in shining armor. When he finally relented, I told him to show me his darkness and he did. I was a sixteen-year-old submissive for six months while I learned what this life was like. I don't hate him for it. He did save me in so many ways. I took to it like a fish to water. And that's where my journey begun.

"Eva, I know we can be good together. We both have demons to overcome, we both need the other to survive, and we can mend our souls by looking to our future. I can't live without you. As dark as my world is, without you, it's like walking through life blind. I need you," Nate implores me. Never did I think I'd see a man like him kneel, beg, or plead. I hold power that I never knew I had with him. All our time together I was always on the receiving end of his dominance.

Now, I have a choice to make.

I look into his eyes, those beautiful pools of dark brown that haunted my dreams over the short time we'd been apart. I was a walking ghost without him, and now I know he felt the same pain I did. "I don't know if I can accept the collar… yet," I say, my voice raspy, my throat dry, aching from screaming at him moments ago. "We need time. I need time, Nate." He nods slowly, relief that I'm not refusing him painting his handsome face.

"Come home with me, Eva?" He asks, his voice low, filled with longing. I don't know if it's a good idea, but staying with Carrick isn't helping matters. "I'll make you dinner, draw you bubble baths and you're welcome to stay in the guest room if you feel you need time. I know I lied. I hid the truth from you, but as we spent more time together, all I wanted was you. Her agreement was null and void by the time I'd asked you to have dinner with me. That was the first date I'd ever had. And when you looked at me with those beautiful eyes, filled with amusement, fire, and yearning, I knew there was no way I was letting you go."

He takes my hand, holding it between both his large ones.

"I'd never dated my slaves. They were merely toys to me. You…" his words trail off, his mind ticking by all the ways he can get me to agree. When he glances up at me again, he continues. "You're the only woman who's gotten into my heart and I can't lose that. Finally, I'm greedy for the right thing. My greed brought me you, and my addiction won't let you leave. I don't know how we're going to land on our feet, but we have to try." He drops his head, looking at my shoes like they're going to give him the answer he seeks.

"You drive a hard bargain, Mr. Ashcroft. Right now,

it feels as if we've just jumped over the ledge and we're currently in a freefall. Let's worry about landing when we get there. Baby steps first," I offer, shutting the velvet box, but holding onto it. "Since this is mine, I'll keep it until we figure out where we stand. If that's okay with you?"

"Anything you want," he smiles, rising to full height, towering over me in his commanding way. His gaze pinning me with not desire, not lust. It bores into me with love.

"Anything?" I quip, my body responding in a completely different way. I don't need the spanking, the toys, or anything else. I only want him and the affection I know he's capable of. Right now, more than anything, I want the sweet, gentle caresses rather than the pain. Tonight, I need the light, in this dark world I've become accustomed to living in. In this lifestyle, there's no way you can stop yourself from forever dousing yourself in the murky shadows. I need it. He does too.

When he finally reaches for me, I fall into his arms. All the while we both stood on our own, but now, we need to stand together. We have a war to fight, a dragon to slay. I never realized how much she hated me, I thought running away would make sure she's out of my life, clearly not.

"Eva, I thought walking away from you was the right thing to do, I did it because I didn't want her hurting you anymore. Fuck, I know I'd done enough damage that night I walked out. But when you told me that Carrick was going to collar you…" He trails off, and I know that must have hurt him as much as I was hurting. "I can't handle it, Eva. I can't lose you."

"You mean you can't handle someone else having me," I murmur under my breath. When I glance up, I see him nod, but doesn't voice his response for so long, I think he's about to change his mind. The cruel way I've always been broken was being reprimanded for wanting something, having it pulled out from under me. And now, even as an adult, I still expect it.

"Knowing another man has you on his arm, in his bed, I can't live with that, Eva."

"Then I can't be with you if you're going to have another woman kneel for you. I may not be a slave, but I'm a submissive. I've always needed the degradation, but from you… From you it feels dishonest. Wrong. I want…" My words trail off because I'm scared. For the first time in a long while I'm afraid of needing someone.

Since I was sixteen I fended for myself. Yes, Carrick was there, but it was always me looking out for myself. No one else mattered. Now though, when I look at Nathan, I'm so fucking scared, I don't know how to do this. How do I finally allow myself to be with someone fully? To give them the ultimate control.

"Eva, you can always tell me what you need or want. I'll change, I'll do anything to have you wear my collar. No more other women, just me and you. We'll set limits, we'll put precautions in place so I'll never do something you don't want."

His sincerity causes my heart to ache. It makes my lungs struggle to breathe. But I look into his eyes when I finally admit what I want from him. "I want you to not only be my Dominant, but I want you to love me too."

TWENTY-ONE

NATE

Her request makes me smile. "Eva." I reach for her face, cupping her cheek gently in my hand. My thumb swipes along her lower lip, causing the light pink gloss to smudge and I imagine making her face streak with makeup while I own her. While I finally take her as mine and collar her.

Her eyes are glistening with unshed tears as we stare at each other for a long while.

"If you can't see by now that I love you, I'll spend each day for the rest of my life showing you. Yes, I want to be your Dominant, but more than that I love you so goddamn much you drive me out of my mind. Never ever question that."

Once again, I swipe my finger along the smooth skin of her cheek, wiping away a fallen tear. I watch her swallow, her lips part, and I wonder what she's about to say. My chest tightens when she reaches for me. Her delicate hand on my face as she regards me with passion so fierce I'm stunned.

"Nate, I love you too." Five words and I know my life is complete. I know that no matter what happens from here, we'll be okay. Things will work out.

"Come home with me," I ask her, lifting my thumb to my mouth, tasting the saltiness of her emotions on my tongue. When she takes a moment to answer, I know the answer will be yes. She doesn't have a choice.

"Okay," she says.

Her response has me releasing a breath I'd been holding in anticipation. Relief sags my shoulders. It won't be long until Marissa comes strolling into my office threatening me, but if I have Eva beside me, I know I'll be able to make it through.

When I pull the door open, I find Carrick glaring at me from the other side. "Are you okay?" His gaze falls on my woman. He doesn't move, as he waits for her response.

"Yes, Rick." She smiles, pulling away from me to circle her arms around him.

I watch him plant a kiss on the top of her head. A friendly gesture, but it still prickles me with jealousy to see how close they are. In a way, I'm glad she had someone to go to when she needed it, but I'm possessive, and from now on, she's mine. Only mine.

He pins me with an angry glare, and utters his warning. "Hurt her again..." I nod before he can say anything more. He doesn't need to tell me what I did, because I know. We'll fight to the death for one woman. I can see he cares for her. It's not love. Not the all-consuming affection that I have for her.

"Thank you, Carrick, for looking after her when I couldn't."

He nods, offering me a hand and releasing my girl. "If you ever need anything..." He smirks in that asshole way he's got. I don't know how he's never found the right woman. Perhaps because he's too much like me in a way. He indulges with too many women, but doesn't allow love into the equation. But for me, there's no more playing with others. I've found my one. The only one I need.

"There might be something you can help me with.

Let me get Eva home and we'll talk later, I'll give you a call," I tell him, our eyes meet in understanding. Carrick has connections in far reaching places. And I have a feeling he's the one who will be able to get Marissa out of our lives for good.

Leading my girl down the hall, I can't help my mind racing with a plan that will once and for all free us from an agreement that I stupidly put myself into. I want that bitch out of my life, but not just mine, Eva's as well. Her body nestles herself into me as we get to the parking lot.

The lights of the car blink twice when I press the key fob. Opening her door, I help Eva into the passenger seat. Rounding the car, I make my way to the driver's side and slip into my seat. Silence lingers as we both figure out what to say. When I glance at her in the seat beside me, I can't help smiling. It's where she belongs.

Her gaze is on me and a soft smile plays on her lips as they quirk into a grin. "I'm tired, Nate."

"We'll be home soon," I say, starting the engine and pulling out onto the road. Home. For me it's always been a place to sleep, to perhaps relax, but it's never been a place I wanted to go after a long day. Which is why I spent my time in casino's, throwing my hard-earned money away.

Now I realize that home is more than just a house with expensive things. It's a place where you feel happiest. A space that allows you to be yourself, and to love yourself. And mine is with her. My home is Eva. With her forgiveness, I feel like I can finally allow myself that luxury. Love.

The drive is silent, the air feels heavy with unsaid words and thoughts. I want to ease her fears, but I don't know how. Pulling into the parking lot, I turn off the engine and exit the car. When I reach her door, I snatch it open, scooping Eva into my arms and carrying her into the elevator. Her face nuzzles into my neck, her steady breaths are calm, warming me all over.

I'd like to play a scene with her, to connect with her, but I think more than anything, I just need to hold her. In the hallway, I manage to get the door open and us inside before slamming it closed with my foot. The place is in darkness as I make my way up to the bedroom—our bedroom—with her.

She's sleeping beside me, no questions asked. There's

no guestroom anymore. This is where she belongs and it's where she'll stay. I lean down, setting her on the soft navy sheet, tugging the comforter over her small frame.

I'm about to say goodnight, but her eyes are already closed, her breathing even, and her body curled into a ball. Her long flowing hair fans over the white pillow making it seem as if she's flying.

She's so goddamn beautiful.

Leaving her, I make my way through to the living room and pull out my phone. I need to talk to Carrick about helping me. If there's one man who can fuck over anyone it's him. I tap the call button and wait. Three rings in, his smooth baritone comes from the other end.

"Nate, calling so soon?"

"Rick, we need to talk. Marissa Gallagher, she's a client of Seven Sins," I start.

"Gallagher?"

"Yeah, she's Eva's mother," I respond, but he sounds as confused as I feel.

He sighs then, frustration clear over the line. "Jesus, will she never learn."

"What do you mean?"

"When I found Eva, she was a runaway. Over time, she trusted me with her past, with who she was. I'd found her mother not long after Eva and I stopped..." He trails off and jealousy burns through my veins. He and my girl were together. I don't need to know that, but he's telling me without words that he's there for her. That he cares.

"Carrick, tell me what the fuck you know."

"Marissa came to me the night you walked in and requested Eva. She spoke to me, gave me some bullshit story that she wanted to sort out things with her daughter. I told her to fuck off, that she no longer had a daughter. I told her to leave my club and I watched her walk out. I didn't realize what her ploy was... She must have wangled her way back in after I left." He explains slowly as realization dawns on us both. I can see his mind racing with thoughts as he rakes his hand through his hair. "The bitch infiltrated my club when I wasn't here. Mason doesn't know her. He has no idea about Eva's past. So, she came to you? She wanted you because of your kink." He says as the truth tumbles free and he sighs.

"I want you to book The Chambers, tell her she has to be there. I'll make sure she talks," I tell him, confident that I know one person who is able to fix this for me. I didn't think about asking him before because he's busy training a new submissive. But it's time I call in the sadist.

"We can do that no problem, but I need to know what you have up your sleeve and I'll do what I can. Marissa isn't stupid, she'll know something's wrong, but right now, I don't give a fuck. I'll call in a favor, have one of my contacts take her out clean." I know he means that offing the bitch would be an option, and as much as I'd enjoy that, it's not going to work. Not for what I have in mind.

"No. We need more, we need leverage," I tell him, urging him to listen to me.

"Okay. How?" Eva isn't going to like it, but if her mother wants to play dirty, I can do that. I can certainly fucking do that. There's only one man I know that can make this work, I need Carrick to provide the venue, and I'll provide the entertainment.

"Oliver Michaelson."

He's silent, and I know he's weighing his options. Either do this and help Eva, or allow the girl he cares for, perhaps a little too much, to walk away. Because there's no doubt, I'll take Eva and run if I have to. I'll cross borders and oceans for her.

I settle at my desk, opening my laptop poised to type an email to the one man I know can manipulate as well as he can defend. The lawyer, and sadist, and one of my best friends.

"Call Oli, I'll set up the room for this weekend," Carrick says, I hear the smile in his tone. He knows as well as I do that this is going to be the death of an ice queen.

"I'll sort it out. Make sure she's in The Chambers at ten on Saturday night. Also," I say, leaning back in my chair as another idea pops into my mind. "Set up three cameras, one in each corner." The room in question is odd shaped, almost triangular, which allows the three cameras to pick up every angle.

"Done. See you then. And Nate," his words halt for a moment. "Don't hurt her again. Or I will be forced to end you."

"Not going to happen, Rick. She's mine now. I love her."

He doesn't say anything before the line dies and I'm typing out an email to my old friend Oli.

TWENTY-TWO

EVA

When I roll over and crack my eyes, I find the darkness wrapped around me like a warm blanket. A soft scent hangs in the air, coffee and cinnamon. Sitting up, I find myself in Nate's bedroom. The silence is beautiful, yet disturbing. The red numbers on his alarm clock tell me it's five in the morning. I must have slept right through.

My body aches from the roller coaster of emotions that've been pulled from me in the last few days. Pulling my hair into a messy bun, I wrap the hair tie around the long strands, and get up. My feet find the plush carpet, reveling in the warmth radiating from the floor.

I'm dressed in only a pair of panties and my bra, so I grab the white robe at the foot end of the bed and shrug it on and make my way toward the door. As soon as I pull it open I'm slammed with the scent of delicious sweet treats. There's a candy scent, with spice, and dark chocolate wafting down the hall. When I step into the kitchen, I find Nathan in only a pair of dark gray boxers, standing at the stove making pancakes.

With his back to me, I can't help watching how the muscles move under the tanned smooth skin. The way they slowly pulse, tightening and releasing, which in turn, causes me to ache with need. It's been a few days since we've been together, too long without him and I miss him.

"Are you going to stand and stare at me all day?" he quips, not bothering to look at me.

"Do you have eyes on the back of your head, Mr. Ashcroft?" I giggle, padding into the kitchen, flopping onto the stool. When he turns around, I notice how his eyes seem to lighten as he meets my gaze.

"I have eyes wherever you are, my beautiful diamond," he utters the words like a vow. A promise that he's not letting me out of his sight again.

"Good," I smile, sitting back, and watching him flip a pancake. Who knew a man as devilish as he is could flip dough in a pan? "How long did I sleep?"

"Seven hours. Since we got home."

"Have you slept at all?" I ask, as he sets a large steamy mug down in front of me filled to the brim with coffee.

"Partially. I've been planning," he responds, planting a chaste kiss on my nose.

"Planning?"

"Carrick and I have a plan. This weekend, we'll get your mother off your back, off my back for good." At the mention of the evil bitch, I can't help shuddering. "Hey," Nate coos and his hands cup my face, making sure I look at him. "She's not going to hurt you anymore."

"I just can't come face to face with her again, Nate."

"You don't have to. If you want to come down to Sins and be there for the scene, you're welcome to. If you don't, then you will stay here."

"Scene? You're doing a scene with her?" I squeak incredulously.

"No, I've got someone who's going to make sure she gets a taste of her own medicine," Nate says proudly. He plants another kiss on me, this time on my lips. The warmth he exudes settles over me causing me to moan.

"Tell me who. I want to know what you're planning."

"Okay. But first, we eat." With a flourish, he turns and finishes up the breakfast he'd been preparing for god knows how long, because when he sets a plate in front of me, it's piled high with pancakes, bacon, scrambled eggs, and tomato.

With my mind still reeling on the plan he's got, I dig into the delicious meal. The thought of seeing my mother again is something I'd been dreading.

One long day has passed and tonight we're setting wheels in motion to free Nate and me from my mother's evil clutches. Stalking into Sins feels different. The long flowing black dress Nathan bought me is incredibly tight and all eyes turn to me as I enter with his arm gently, yet possessively wrapped around me. His fingertips graze the bare skin where the dress has been cut out against my hip, to show off my smooth tanned curves.

"You look beautiful, Sweet Slut," Nate murmurs against my ear, causing me to tremble with an ache that tightens my belly. He's in role. I'm his pet in here.

"And you look handsome, Sir," I utter, my voice dropping low so only he can hear me. We reach the bar, and I offer Dylan a smile.

"Hey, chicka," he smiles. His face lighting up when he sees me on Nate's arm. Dylan has been here for far too long not to know what the clients are like. I'm sure he's heard the stories that have filtered to me from the other toys that Nathan's taken. Only this time, I know things are different.

"Have a bottle of your finest champagne delivered to the back room of The Chambers, we have a private party." Dylan nods at Nate's command and we turn to find Mason and Savvie on stage. Her beautiful blonde hair shimmers like gold as she twirls in the air.

"And that is our show for this evening. I trust you enjoyed it and we hope to see you again soon," Mason smirks, bowing to the audience.

"Do you want to do that?" Nate whispers in my ear as we head down the hallway to where tonight's show is about to play out in one of the darkest scenes I'll witness. I don't know if I'll stomach it, but from what I've heard of Oliver Michaelson, he's a savage.

"Maybe, I love the rope." My voice is low. I know Nathan is trying to distract me, but now that we're here, the anxiety twirls in my stomach.

As soon as we step into the viewing room, I come face to face with a handsome man, a silver fox if you must. His full head of salt and pepper hair has more gray than black, but his face is young looking. He's dressed in a pinstripe black suit. A silver shirt and black tie under the dark jacket pop in the dimly lit room. Soft red lighting seems to make him look scarier.

He's tall, probably over six-feet. With his hands in the pockets of his suit pants, he turns his green stare on us. "Nathan," he says, oozing sex, danger, and pure vengeance in his smirk. If someone could make me cower, it would be him. His clean shaven rigid jaw is angular, with a sharp nose, and severe expression, shows that this man means business.

"Oli," Nate shakes his hand which causes Oliver to smile. He actually grins and I'm trapped in his lure. Small dimples at the edge of his mouth appear, showing off a handsome man that I'm sure would have any woman, or man, falling to their knees.

His gaze falls on me, pinning me with a sinful stare that almost has my knees buckling. He reaches for my hand, his touch is gentle, commanding, and utter dominance. "Pleased to meet you, Sweet Slut," he breathes, his lips find my knuckles and heat sizzles through me.

"That's enough, Oli," the man beside me, my Dominant, growls. Once this handsome stranger releases me, I'm tugged into Nate's arms. "Go do your job and quit trying to steal my submissive." The warning earns Sir a chuckle, but he doesn't respond. Merely bows and heads out the door and into the main room.

TWENTY - THREE

NATE

When I look at Eva, I know she's enamored with him. Oliver has a way of weaving a spell around anyone. That's why, man or woman, he's had them all at his feet.

When I met Oliver in college, he took me under his wing teaching me the ways of being a Dominant. Even though I'm not a sadist like him, I find that he understood my need for humiliation. He got to the root of my problem. When I was younger, I'd been through it, humiliated because of my upbringing, of who I was. Not exactly the most popular kid in school.

That in turn slowly led me down this sordid path that's now turned into something sexual. That's how I found my outlet. To do it to someone else. Namely a beautiful woman. And strangely, when I found out how many women wanted that treatment, I was shocked.

Oliver, now in his early forties still has the grace, the

charm, and that dominant streak that causes men and women to turn their heads when he walks into a room. For years, I'd confided in him. When I told him about Emilia, he responded with *"I knew it,"* shocking me. Apparently, he'd seen that she wasn't what I needed, but I was so damn blind to her that I was deaf to any advice.

He told me that he wanted to let me play it out. In this lifestyle, it's intense, emotions run high. It's deeper, more emotional than any other 'normal' relationship because you're not only loving someone, you're giving them full control over your body, mind, and soul. Ultimate submission. That's why a lot of the time submissives become overly attached. They think it's love when it's merely need.

Eva cuts through my thoughts when she speaks. "Have you…? I mean—"

"No, Eva. I haven't fucked Oliver. I've watched him with both men and women, but never have I been with him," I tell her, pulling her into the crook of my arm. She looks utterly sinful tonight. The dress hugs every inch of her—all those tiny nooks I want to devour.

"Okay, I was curious," she says watching him set

up the room. There are whips, canes, even a small bench which I know he's going to use to bind her to. He is the perfect man to pull the information from her. To make her feel safe, then really punish her. Something tells me he's going to enjoy this a lot more than he should.

There's something about the false sense of security he's going to give her and then suddenly rip the blanket out from under her feet. It's that agony I hope will make her see what a sick individual she is. My guilt is still something I'm dealing with, all those girls she told me to degrade, to humiliate, didn't deserve it. They didn't ask for it. But I did it to save myself.

I've made a decision which I still need to talk to Eva about. Giving up this life and moving away is the first step to a fresh start. Something I need. Something that I want to give Eva because I know she deserves more than this place. More than the memories that will linger every time we walk into Seven Sins.

I want to make her forget her past so she can look forward to a new future. One with me. Where she can be anything she wants to be. I'll do anything for her. I'm changing myself to keep the woman I love and I couldn't be happier. When I fell to my knees, for her it dawned on me, she is it. I'd never knelt for another woman. I'd never given myself so wholly to anyone. Not even Emelia.

Eva came into my life, I walked into hers, and slowly we've both changed. She's slowly accepting the way I like things. And even though I no longer bring other women into our scenes, there's still a lot of other things we have to enjoy. She loves when I take her the way I need. I degrade her, but I love her. She knows it and that's the difference. She looks into my soul, into the depths of my depravity and she loves my monster that lurks beneath the surface. Something that no one ever has done before.

The door to the viewing room opens and the waiter sets the champagne on the table. Once we're alone again, I turn to Eva. "I want you to experience anything you want in this lifestyle. I'm here as your protector, your partner, but most importantly, I'm your Dominant," I utter, trailing my fingertips over her arms. The skin prickles with goosebumps at my touch which makes me smile. "I'm meant to push your limits. Those boundaries are meant to be shoved and broken. Each time we play a scene, I want it to be memorable. And I meant what I said, I will change for you. No more other women, unless you're comfortable. But don't doubt, I'll degrade you in all the deliciously decadent ways, my Sweet Slut."

I lean in, planting a soft kiss on her lips. They mold to mine in the most perfect way. She's mine, I shouldn't have walked away, but this time, she's not going anywhere. Our tongues dance as I lick into her mouth, tasting her sweetness. A groan rumbles in my throat when she sucks on my tongue, like she would my cock, taunting me and I feel myself thicken, needy for her.

I'd love to shove her against the wall and take her, but soon we'll have Carrick here and he's the last person I want seeing Eva naked ever again. Pressing her against the wall with my body, I roll my hips, allowing her to feel my hardness. "This is what you always do to me. I want to fuck you right here, right now. I want to make you cry out as I violate your sweet tight cunt, but that will have to wait," I tease, pulling away leaving her cheeks flushed, and her breaths coming out in ragged gasps.

"You're insufferable." Her retort only earns her a chuckle. She's cute when she's angry. I know I love her.

This isn't a passing faze, it's real. I feel it down to my very soul. This woman is my forever, and I'll make sure she knows it every day of her life.

When the door opens again, we're met with Carrick. He glances between us, nodding at me, but his concentration is on Eva. On my woman.

"How are you, Eva?" he asks, ignoring me.

"I'm good," she responds. Her gaze flitting between us. "You two need to stand down. This isn't a pissing contest. And it's definitely not a place to compare the size of your dicks." My woman is feisty. Two completely dominant men and she's telling us what to do.

"Sit," I tell her, and she obeys. Not a moment too soon the door in the main room opens and her mother walks into the Chamber, along with a young man that can't be more than twenty. It seems Marissa knows Oliver's penchant for men. Which makes me wonder if she's done her research on the room we're using.

Even if she did, she wouldn't know about the camera's set up, filming both her confession, and her being used like a toy. She deserves everything Oliver is going to give her. And more. But for now, all we need is her giving us the truth about what she did with Eva's inheritance.

TWENTY - FOUR

EVA

The man my mother walks in with is young looking. He's probably my age, early twenties with messy golden hair, blue eyes the color of the sky, and a lean frame. She's dressed in a red pencil skirt and jacket to match, with a black blouse underneath.

"I've brought you a toy, Oliver. This is Trey. I've heard you like them young. He's just turned twenty-one," she says. Her voice is cold—void of any emotion—just like I remember. "Sit," her order is harsh as she spits it toward the young man.

"Thank you, Marissa. You're very kind, but tonight, we're playing by my rules. Will you obey me?" Oliver's deep rumble comes over the speakers. My mother nods. "Good." He stalks to the young man, reaching for his face, he cups it in his large hand and leans in to plant a kiss on the other man's lips. The sight of two men kissing turns me on; my nipples harden as I watch their tongues duel, their bodies flush against each other. And it causes me to wonder what they'd look like naked. Two hard bodies, two cocks.

"Are you enjoying the show, Sweet Slut?" Nate murmurs in my ear.

"Yes," I rasp, my voice husky.

"Perhaps one day Oli will allow you to watch him. He does love an audience." The illicit promise sends heat between my legs, and I squeeze my thighs together. When their kiss breaks, Oliver turns a sinful smirk our way before turning back to my mother.

"Your kink for dominating, but sitting on the sidelines is something of a talent, Marissa," he says, leaving the younger man flushed.

"What can I say? I like to watch."

Oliver nods, stalking toward the door, he opens it and there waiting on the other side is a brunette, she's my height, her curves almost match mine and her eyes, they're the same hue as mine. She could be my sister. "I have a little pet for you to play with, I know you like young girls," he says, turning to face my mother as he pulls the submissive into the room.

My gaze snaps to Nate, and then Carrick; I know the concern is etched on my face because both men give either of my shoulders a reassuring squeeze.

As they continue their scene, my mother sits back on the sofa, and orders the young man to guide his cock into the submissives mouth. "Deeper. Do it like you want to break her," she bites out. It's vile, and I find myself hiding my face in the crook of Nathan's neck. The sounds of a girl choking echo around us and I find tears springing to my eyes.

"Stop," Oliver commands and all sounds cease. "Time for me to play. Marissa, strip, now," he says in a no-nonsense tone. I watch as she smirks evilly at the man ordering her around. There's no denying him. He's in full on Dominant mode and a fearful shudder shoots through me. When I glance back at the room, my mother is now standing in a black leather corset, her panties match. I'm morbidly fascinated by what Oliver is about to do as he grabs her wrist, pulling her over to a bench which I recognize as a spanking bench.

No words are spoken. She follows his instruction as

he bends her over with a sneer. He continues to bind her to the contraption. "I don't see what the point of this is, Oliver. I mean—" Before she can finish her sentence, he lifts the whip that was lying on the bed and brings it down on her legs.

"You see, Marissa, a good friend gave me a call," Oli speaks in a tone so calm, it's as if he's telling a bedtime story. He's behind her, nudging his chin he orders the other two out of the room. Once the lock clicks, he brings the whip down on her again.

"Oliver."

Ignoring her plea, he continues. "You've been a bad person all your life." Another harsh swat and I see her arms and legs tugging at the metal restraints. "Me. I'm a vile person, I love inflicting pain." SWAT. "And when I do, it brings me joy, especially when I know that the person is deserving of it." He drops the whip, picks up a cane, and even I cringe.

The wooden cane is not to be taken lightly. I've seen what it can do. He lifts it, and brings it down on her panty covered ass. Seeing my mother cry is something otherworldly. The menacing sound of the bamboo swishing through the air sounds like a serpent ready to attack.

Again and again.

Another and another.

Each time her screeches get louder. Her pain resonates through the room. A living force.

"My friend, Nathan said that you've been doing things that are… possibly illegal. Tell me about them," he says, it's such a gentle sound compared to the way he's attacking her. "Tell me, Marissa, I won't ask again." He halts the lashings for a moment and then I hear it.

I hear the confession.

"I wanted to hurt Evangeline because she's not my daughter. I met her father when she was only a year old. Her mother died in childbirth. I fell in love with him. He was everything to me, but she…she was always his fucking light. I was second to her and I hated it." The venom she spits her words with courses through my veins. She's not my mother. All these years I cried for the love of a woman, I hated a woman who I thought was a mother and she was nothing more than a gold-digging whore.

"You wanted her gone? You had her brutally assaulted by your piece of shit partner, who by the way, is in the room beside us. A friend of mine is having some fun with him." When Oliver picks up a blade, fear grips me.

"What is he doing?" I ask, glancing at Nathan who's enraptured by the scene before us. "Carrick?" I turn to my best friend.

"Don't worry, sweetheart," Carrick answers me, but his eyes are glued to Oliver in the room.

"Tell me, Marissa. Did you enjoy seeing her violated?" Oli runs the blade over her corset, pushing the tip into her flesh and then I see a trickle of crimson. "I love knife play, it's so dangerous. I mean… if you move, I could hurt you severely. Couldn't I, Marissa?"

"Please, stop this. I've told you why I did it."

"Now you'll tell me where all that money you stole from her is hidden." He taunts, as the knife trails down to her core. I know if she just so much as wriggles it's going to be painful.

"I-I… Oliver, please?"

"That's not the answer." His gaze lifts to the mirror

and it's as if he's looking directly at me. The corner of his mouth lifts into a smirk, his eyes that are a beautiful shade of gray glass, are now a stormy sky.

"I-I, there's an account. I'll give you the information." The woman whimpers as I watch him trail the knife up to her material covered ass, and press the tip of the blade in. Her screech is the only evidence that he's pierced skin.

"Small pin pricks won't scar. But where you're going… well, let's just say they don't care about scars." Then he places the knife on the table and shrugs on his jacket. "I'll have my men get the account details from you. Make no mistake. If you lie, we'll know and you'll have to endure much more of this."

He sets the knife down and I watch her visibly exhale.

"Now," Oliver says, rolling the sleeves of his shirt up his thick arms. Once they're both up to his elbows, he unties her and drags her over to another wooden contraption. "You know what this is. Don't you?" His voice is filled with an underlying rage. The restraint he wields is that of utter perfection. Silently, he positions her on the thin wooden beam, legs either side.

"What is that?" I ask, looking at Nate.

"It's a riding bench. It's one of the torture devices used on naughty slaves." His answer causes me to shudder. The word torture turns my blood cold.

"Look, Oliver—" Marissa starts, but her words are cut short when Oli tugs the chain lifting the wooden beam between her legs causing her to screech again. The wood looks sharp, almost as if it's cutting between her thighs.

"I do love the riding bench. It requires strength. Something not a lot of slaves possess," the older man says with a satisfied grin. She lifts onto her tiptoes, clearly needing reprieve from the device, but like Oliver said, you need strength. "Ride it!" He orders then, lifting the whip and once again swatting her thighs with the leather.

When she drops onto the wood, her hips move slowly as she obeys Oliver. I realize Nathan was right, he's indeed a sadist.

"I'm going to make you bleed, Marissa. I love seeing skin dotted with the beautiful crimson."

"Do it. I should have had those men teach Eva a lesson. I didn't realize she was into all this. Perhaps they could have made her worth something. She could have earned me more money with her slut holes." She cackles as her words cause bile to rise in my stomach. Without another word, I push off the chair hastily and race to the door. It's enough. Shoving the restroom door open, I make it to the cubicle in time to empty the contents of my stomach.

"Eva," Nate's worried voice comes from behind me. "Baby, I'm sorry. I didn't—"

"It's not you. I just can't believe she's still so hateful. Even in her torment." He helps me wipe my mouth, and then pulls me into an embrace that both warms and calms me.

"It's over now, my love. It's over."

His words soothe, but the endearment has my heart fluttering wildly in my chest. It really is over.

We walked side by side into war. Now that we've won, I want the life I was always meant to live. I want the happiness she stole from me, and I know with Nate I'll have it.

EVA

When I glance up from my laptop, I notice Nate stalking back and forth wearing a hole into the carpet. "Babe, sit down," my voice travels to him in a soft murmur. When he snaps his gaze to mine, I can see the startling brown that is mostly hidden when he's stressed. Today is the first day of his new job. After allowing Asher to take over A&B Finance fully, Nathan decided to go into business with Mason and Carrick. Three headstrong men in one business will be one hell of a feat. Nate will be running the Los Angeles club, and since we moved four months ago, we've spent our time getting used to the area before the opening.

It's so different from Chicago, the weather is incredible and my new job is perfect. As soon as we arrived, I applied for a position at one of the smaller boutique online magazines. Using a pseudonym, I write a weekly advice column on the lifestyle. I answer any questions people, especially submissives, have. When there's a question I can't advise on, Nathan helps me form a male perspective. I'm excited and delighted to be able to help someone who's new and scared, just like I was.

By night, I write my columns, but by day, I work as a model for a lingerie company offering beautiful timeless underwear. It's an elegant, yet sexy line and I'm proud to be the face of it. I don't see myself doing it forever, but for now, I'm loving it.

"I've been on the phone for an hour with the supplier. He's still trying to find the velvet I asked for," Nate grunts in frustration. Rising from the seat, I pad over to him. Our office is at the back of the house, overlooking the infinity swimming pool and the Hollywood sign.

"Babe." My hands find his shoulders bunched up and tense. "Look at me," I order. We've slowly become more at ease with each other, working through our needs and wants. There are times he needs my control, but mostly, I'm under his. Which I love. Relinquishing everything to him is freeing.

His eyes meet mine, they burn through me, finding my soul and gripping it tightly. Immediately, I sink to my knees, looking at his bare feet on the soft white carpet. "Eva," he whispers. We've played before over the past few weeks. But today he needs more. "I can't—"

"You can, Master. Let me be your slut," I utter the words he craves.

"Look at me," he orders, immediately falling into his role. Lifting my eyes, I meet his, recognizing how they've darkened to almost black. Dark desire swims in depths of his gaze, pinning me in place. "If I take you now, I'll fuck you. It will be brutal."

"Do it. I told you, I want you. This," I gesture between us. "Is us. It will always be us. I need you to use me, and you need me to relax."

"Good girl. Go to the playroom, I want you on the floor beside the tower." I nod. Rising without a word, I head to the room in question. On the upper level of our apartment, it sits, beckoning me. As soon as I step inside, I sigh in relief. Stripping off, I leave my clothes beside the door and kneel as requested beside the tower. The long steel pole is attached to the floor and ceiling.

It has a spreader bar for my feet which keeps me open and exposed to Nate's ministrations. The cuffs that are attached to it are to keep my hands close to my hips, but behind me and a collar which holds me firmly in place.

The door clicks; his cologne wafts through the room, enveloping me in his scent. "Position yourself, sweet slut." His command comes quickly.

I rise, stepping onto the metal plate with my limbs in place at the restraints. Nate is wearing a pair of charcoal sweats. They don't hide the thick erection he's sporting. He binds me to the metal pole. Once he's happy with his work, he lifts the white wand and smiles at me.

"Orgasm torture is my favorite way to pass the time," he murmurs, leaning in, allowing his mouth to tease my earlobe. His teeth graze the flesh sending a shudder through me. He attaches the wand to the clamp and places it on my clit. "If you make a noise, you'll get double. Do you understand?"

"Yes, Sir," I utter nervously. Some may think orgasms aren't a form of torture, but when you're forced to come ten or more times in a row, there's nothing that can make you beg for more.

"Good girl." The two words that leave me utterly his. He fastens the cuffs around my wrists, the collar slides around my neck, then my ankles get locked in place with thick black metal. Finally, he turns on the Wand, the soft vibration on my clit is incredible. Gently at first, but I know with seven settings I'll soon be begging him to stop. I watch him move around the room exuding dominance as he goes. He picks his favorite flogger, stalks toward me and stops, legs spread, his chest heaving already. "You're my special girl," he tells me with admiration. "It's been an adjustment after all the shit that happened... And you know why I'm so tense, sweet slut?"

He raises the leather, bringing it down on my tits, my stomach, and my legs while the wand teases my clit mercilessly. The pain and pleasure shoot through me causing me to whimper. My nerves are frayed in the best way, tingling through my body.

"Answer me!"

"No, Sir. I don't know why you're so tense," I say quietly before he lashes me with a new round of swats causing me to moan and plead for more. My body trembles, needy and wet for him. When he finally drops the flogger, his lips find mine in a searing kiss, warming me, tempting me, taunting me. He breaks the kiss, meeting my gaze and I finally ask. "Tell me, please?"

He grins, turning the wand up two notches. The jolt to my clit is intense, breaking through the lust and sending me over the edge as my body pulses with an orgasm so strong I cry out in pleasure.

I feel my arousal dripping down my thighs, but I can't do anything about it.

"You haven't put my collar on," he grunts, twisting up the wand another notch, and my hardened nub tingles as the tension leaves my body limp.

"I can't… Please?"

"Can't put the collar on?" he taunts. He knows what he's doing. Torturing me with too much pleasure which doesn't allow me to function properly. I can't speak. I can't think.

"No, I… Orgasm…" My words are mumbled, falling from my lips and not making sense. "Please?"

"Do you want me inside you, sweet slut?" he asks, his face close to mine, his fingers teasing my wet core.

The buzzing on my clit hasn't stopped and my mind feels blank. "Look at me," he murmurs softly. He dips two fingers inside me. Our gazes lock—his black with lust, mine teary with need.

"Fuck me, Sir. Please?"

Swiftly, the buzzing stops, the clamp is moved somehow, and in second I'm filled beyond measure. Even though I'm drenched, feeling him enter me is like finding a piece of me that was missing. He completes the broken parts of me as I heal the shattered pieces of him.

Our bodies are fluid. Our mouths are glued in passion, yearning, and desire.

"Oh, God!" I cry out as his finger finds my puckered entrance, dipping inside me while his cock claims me.

"Tell me, Eva?"

"What? Please?"

"Tell me you'll wear it?" He grunts with each thrust. Every word a drive, a plunge deeper, hitting my soul.

"Yes! Yes! Please, let me come!"

"Do it. Mark me, sweet slut. And I'll keep you as mine."

And I do. Our bodies lock, as do our hearts, and I

know I'm forever branded to him.

PLAYLIST

- Take Me To Church - Hozier

- Beast Within - In This Moment

- It's Not Over - Daughter

- Better than Me - Hinder

- Ride - Chase Rice

- Whisper - Chase Rice

- Hello - Adele

- Hurricane - Thirty Seconds To Mars

- Passenger Side - Jay Sean

- Closer To You - Adelitas Way

- Roulette - Katy Perry

- Let Her Go - Passenger

- Earned it - The Weeknd

- Hate It When You See Me Cry - Halestorm

- Bottoms Up - Brantley Gilbert

- A Thousand Years - Christina Perri

ACKNOWLEDGMENTS

This is always the most difficult part of writing. At least, I find it is because there are so many amazing people who are instrumental in bringing the book to life.

Firstly, I need to thank my BETAs. You ladies LOVED Nate even though he can be an asshole. Thank you for embracing him and Eva and giving me feedback. Your words of encouragement and never-ending support are the foundation behind my words. So, Tam, Cat, Sheena, Becca, Melissa, thank you for everything!

My super awesome babe and editor, Shana, thank you for taking time out of your insane schedule to polish up the story. Your input is always appreciated and I can't thank you enough for everything.

My Decadent Dolls street team—Tre, Sheena, Sarah, Tamara, Becca, Lisa, Susan, Dawn, TJ—thank you for pimping my work EVERYWHERE. You ladies rock!!

My reader group, The Darklings, you ladies keep me sane.

Every day I pop in there and I'm always blown away by all of you. Joy and Oindrilla's daily funnies make sure I have my daily dose of laughs. I'm so grateful to have a place to go to when I need to smile.

To all my author colleagues, thank you for always sharing, commenting, and supporting me. I appreciate every one of you. Having a support system is important and you ladies provide that and so much more.

Readers and bloggers, from the bottom of my little black heart, THANK YOU. All you do for us authors is incredible. Reading and reviewing is demanding on your own time and you do it with a smile. Thank you so, so much. You are valued and appreciated for taking time out to show us so much love.

A SNEAK PEEK AT
OBEY

PROLOGUE

GIANA

It's been weeks since I saw him. Since the moment I laid eyes on the tall, dark and handsome man, I knew I wanted him. My memory is crystal clear. It's him. It's always been him, only I can't go to him and tell him who I am, so I watch him from afar. He walks into the store with his briefcase in hand every day, dressed in an Armani suit that is tailored for him. I know this because there's no secrets between us. At least, there never used to be.

Elijah Draydon.

Thirty-six-year-old billionaire with a seemingly perfect life. At least, that's what it looks like from where I'm standing. With eyes the color of gold, dark hair that's tousled in such a way I wonder if he fucks just before he walks into the store. And lips that curl perfectly into a Cupid's bow. Full, pink, and delicious.

His five o'clock shadow is barely there, the dark dusting just visible, making sure my thighs squeeze together in that needy way I'm sure most women do when they look at him. Everything about him screams sex; he exudes it like it's part of his personality. I have no doubt that when he sheds that designer suit, it's exactly what he's good at. Making women come so hard they forget their own name. I just wish I could be one of those again. I was once, only he doesn't know it. He won't recognize me because I don't look the same. I've changed my hair, I no longer have those god-awful braces, and I've grown into a woman. Years have passed, and even now when I look at him, I recall every moment his fingers touched my body, and the way his lips would devour my cunt.

Each morning, I serve his coffee and at every lunch time I make sure his Caesar salad is free of croutons. But he doesn't know who I am, he doesn't recognize me.

My job at Mocha Coffees is only my day job. It's at night that I see Eli in a completely different light. In the way I remember him.

When he walks into the nightclub where I work the bar, that's when he's in his element. Dressed in dark jeans and a smart dress shirt, he still looks as well put together as he does in the daylight hours, the only difference is what he's drinking, and the entertainment he enjoys.

Beautiful women flock to him while he sits at the bar. Out of all the hundreds of plastic Barbie dolls that drape themselves over him, he'll choose one to take home. I've heard stories about his dungeon. I've also heard about his penchant for rope, pain, and choking.

"Good morning, Giana."

The deep rumble of his voice is enough to have my panties wet. Glancing up, I find the man in question standing before me with a smirk on his face. "Good morning. The usual?" He nods, then drops those golden eyes to his phone. As I make the Americano, I steal glances at his fingers, remembering how they felt pleasuring me.

Clearing my throat, I set the cup down. "Thank you." Another smirk. He offers me the note and grabs the mug. "Keep the change." With that, he leaves me staring at his beautiful form. One day, Mr. Draydon. One day soon.

SINS OF SEVEN

READ MORE ABOUT THE OTHER COUPLES IN THE SERIES

Kneel (Book #1)

Obey (Book #2)

Indulge (Book #3)

Ruthless (Book #4)

Bound (Book #5)

Envy (Book #6)

Vice (Book #7)

ABOUT DANI

Dani is a *USA Today* bestselling author of a variety of genres, from romantic suspense to dark erotic romance and even BDSM romance. She loves to delve into the raw, emotional journeys her characters venture on, and enjoys the dark, edgy, and sensual scenes that fill the pages of her books. Dani's stories are seductive with a deviant edge with feisty heroines and dominant alphas.

Dani lives in the beautiful city of Cape Town, and is a proud member of the Romance Writer's Organization of South Africa (ROSA) and the Romance Writers of America (RWA). She has a healthy addiction to reading, TV series, music, tattoos, chocolate, and ice cream.

www.danirene.com

info@danirene.com

FIND DANI ONLINE

Do you follow me?

If not, head over to any of the below links,

I love to hear from my readers!

Amazon

BookBub

Facebook

Facebook Group

Goodreads

Twitter

Pinterest

Instagram

Website & Store

Newsletter

Spotify

OTHER BOOKS

STAND ALONES

Choosing the Hart

Love Beyond Words

Cuffed

Fragile Innocence

Perfectly Flawed

Black Light: Obsessed

Among Ash and Ember

Within Me (Limited Time)

Cursed in Love (collaboration with Cora Kenborn)

Beautifully Brutal (Cavalieri Della Morte)

TABOO NOVELLAS

Sunshine and the Stalker (collaboration with K Webster)

His Temptation

Austin's Christmas Shortcake

Crime and Punishment (Newsletter Exclusive)

Malignus (Inferno World Novella)

Virulent (collaboration with Yolanda Olson)

Tempting Grayson